S.G. PUBLISH

THE UNGODLY PASTOR

A WORK OF FICTION

COUNTRY MCRAE & BOOG DENIRO

★ BOOG DENIRO ★

RESPECT THE STRUGGLE

TO RESPECT THE STRUGGLE YOU MUST UNDERSTAND THE STRUGGLE

STREET GENERALS 1,

NO SELLOUTS

STREET GENERALS II,

NOTHING IS SACRED

STREET GENERALS III,

CAN'T STOP WON'T STOP

S.G. PUBLISHING PRESENTS…

Email: sgpublishingllc@gmail.com

ISBN 13 – 9 7 8 – 0 – 9 8 2814 4 – 5 – 1
ISBN10 – 0 – 9 8 2814 4 – 5 – 3

Authors: Country MCRae & BOOG DENIRO
Editor: BOOG DENIRO
Typeset: BOOG DENIRO

First Trade Paperback Edition Printing
10 9 8 7 6 5 4 3 2 1
Printed in the USA

Genesis 1: Verses 3 and 4

And God said, "Let there be light," and there was light. God saw that the light was good, and he separated the light from the darkness.

S.G. PUBLISHING PRESENTS…

THE UNGODLY PASTOR

Chapter 1

Pushing his charcoal gray Lincoln Navigator through the busy traffic down Roxboro Road, 53-year old Reverend Earl Reeves listened intently to the "*Greatest Songs*" of Rick James cd, as it played from the speakers of his Yamaha sound system.

It was a Saturday and he was on his way to get one of his many tailor made suits from the Stacy Adams store. Located in the Northgate Mall, it was one of the O.G. stores in Durham, N.C. Most of the local preachers and pastors shopped there.

Making a left on Club Blvd, the Reverend could see the mall from a distance. Scanning the busy parking lots and decks as he continued to cruise, he couldn't recall the last time he saw so many people in one place.

"Daaaaamn…I should've came out here earlier," he mouthed, glancing at the gold and diamond Rolex beautifying his left wrist. It was 2:15 in the evening. In the south, anything after noon was considered *the evening*. At that time of the day, the mall was jumping, but never that much.

Slowing down, and taking the far right lane to turn up into the mall's parking lot entrance, Reverend Reeves noticed a woman in a 2016 gold Toyota Camry backing out of a parking spot close to the food court.

"Praise the Lord," he stated as he hurried towards the spot and watched the car back out. "God, you are good to me."

Reverend Reeves always praised God whenever a come up was involved. He had more game than LeBron James.

Once the car pulled off, the Reverend zipped his whip into the empty space. Taking his time as Rick James crooned "*Super Freak*", he turned the ignition off. Reverend Reeves did a thorough onceover of the inside of the exclusive SUV. To hide the blunt that was half smoked, he closed the ashtray. Reaching into an open compartment that sat under the ashtray, the Reverend grabbed his old school Drakkar cologne. With his iced out pointer finger, he pumped the spray nozzle.

Spppppp—he hit his neck.

Spppppp—he hit his chest.

Reverend Reeves sprayed anywhere that he felt would hide the aroma of the killer exotic he had been puffing on.

Reaching for the door handle, he looked into the mirror. "Yeah, I better drop some Visine," he muttered to himself as he reached for the Visine that also sat in the open compartment.

He squeezed a drop of the clear solution in each eye. Reaching into the inside of his brown Tom Ford blazer, Revered Reeves pulled out a silk white handkerchief. Looking into the mirror, he examined his eyes and wiped the wetness from the corners. Feeling that he was now up to par, Reverend Reeves put the Visine and cologne back into the compartment and slipped from the driver's side door.

Reverend Reeves shut the door, and checked out his

swag from head to toe. From his blazer to his feet, Reverend Reeves was a medium build with a little muscle tone to his stature. The bald head hid his receding hairline, and he kept his beard low and lined up to the max. To be 53, Revered Reeves was a handsome man who attracted women of various ages ranging from 25 on up.

Even though he sat in the pulpit with his wife, "The First Lady", the women of Jubilee Baptist Church threw themselves at the Reverend on a regular basis. Some did so by jumping up and down just so that their breasts would bounce to entice him, while other women fainted just so that they could fall to the floor in front of the Reverend with their legs splayed showing their treat meat. All they wanted the reverend to do was lay hands, and he loved every single minute of it.

Walking in his signature stride, Reverend Reeves headed towards the mall. He could feel the adoration of women, and the envy of men checking him out as the Reverend waited for traffic to pass before crossing the mall's busy intersection, neither stronger than the other. Serving God was one thing, but that was what he really lived for. The Reverend loved the attention.

Moving quickly, his brown alligator shoes touched the other side of the street and landed on the sidewalk as he made his way towards the mall's entrance. His necklace and diamonds glistened once he made his grand entrance. Looking around at the busy food court, Reverend Reeves smiled. From Chic-Fi-la, The Wong Fe, and all the other eating spots, women were everywhere.

Out of the blue, he heard someone calling his name.

"Hey, Reverend Reeves. Over here!!!" the feminine voice chimed out over all the noise.

With his eyes, the Reverend searched through the crowded place to see who was seeking his attention.

Having surfed the crowd for nearly two minutes, he spotted the woman the lovely voice belonged to. It was Mrs. Marjorie Brown. She was a very beautiful woman who had just celebrated her 63rd birthday. Also, she was in charge of his usher board at Jubilee Baptist.

Marjorie had not too long ago became a widow. She was sitting at one of the dining tables in front of Baskin Robbins all alone. Since Marjorie's husband's violent death, and she being the sole beneficiary, Reverend Reeves knew that Mrs. Marjorie was a true candidate for a quick come up.

"Praaaisse the Lord!!" he bellowed with enthusiasm and made his way over to Mrs. Marjorie.

She sat in a position that flattered her pretty and thick legs that were extending from beneath a denim skirt that she wore by DOLCE & GABBANA.

Marjorie was a red-bone with brown naturally curly tresses. Her green eyes sat behind her gold rimmed Tory Burch frames. To be her age, Marjorie was thick to def. She could've easily been mistaken for Lynn Whitfield. Being so fine and thick, Marjorie attracted a lot of younger men in the church, and pretty much anywhere else she traveled.

Definitely, she was on Reverend Reeves' radar for quite some time. Being a retired Administrative assistant for Blue Cross – Blue Shield, and coming up on her husband's assets, ever since he preached her husband's funeral, Reverend Reeves was seeking ways to get into Marjorie's panties. She was sure enough good as a ton of platinum in Reverend Reeves' eyes.

"As I walk down the road of darkness and despair, suddenly I see the light of an angel," he said, as he extended his arms out for a warm embrace. "For some reason God has allowed for you to be that beacon of light. Because … I was feeling weary, Marjorie."

"That's how the Lord operates," she replied in an understanding and empathetic tone, as she stood and hugged the Reverend. "He knows when his people are in need."

Rubbing his hands gently across her back, feeling the fabric of Marjorie's yellow blouse, Reverend Reeves could feel his Johnson rocking up.

"Let's have a seat," the Reverend insisted while releasing the embrace.

Quickly, he sat down at the table and slid the chair close to it. Reverend Reeves didn't want to stand and talk because now he was bone hard and Marjorie would've definitely taken notice.

The Reverend had a thousand things going through his mind, all of which he wanted to do in the bed with Marjorie.

"So what are you doing at this busy place on a Saturday, at this time of the evening at that? Shouldn't you be preparing for your sermon tomorrow?"

Looking into Marjorie's eyes, Reverend Reeves replied, "When God is doing the talking there is nothing to prepare for. His word flows and soothes our souls through me."

"Ammmen...to that!" she rejoiced as if Reverend reeves was preaching then. "I can't wait to hear the word tomorrow."

To himself Reverend Reeves thought, *Me either. You and the ushers just have them baskets ready to get that damn paper.*

"Oooh...It's going to be an awesome sermon. I got to lead the flock to green pastures," he eventually verbalized, further moving Marjorie. "But to answer your question; I came out here to pick up a suit that I had tailored."

"Really ...I'm doing the same. Reverend Reeves, I got to pick up a dress from Macy's," Marjorie stated in a surprised tone. "I guess we can hang out together and have a shopping revival."

Reverend Reeves sat and thought to himself as he held a half smile, *Is you paying for my shit???*

The Reverend was straight with paper, on many fronts. He didn't need anyone paying his tabs. But entitlement was one of his character flaws he just couldn't shake.

Holding Marjorie's hand gently, he decided to say, "That sounds great. I'm going to the Stacey Adams store. That's right by Macy's."

Feeling the Reverend release her hand, and watching him rise from the table, she said, "I'm honored to be in your company. The only time that we normally talk is at church or the meetings. Reverend Reeves it's a blessing for us to be able to converse outside the church in our normal everyday life."

Marjorie then got up from the table also. "While we're shopping you can share with me what you're going through Reverend."

Reaching for her purse that hung on the left arm of the chair, Reverend Reeves was sweating Marjorie's thickness as she leaned over.

Yessss, Looord!, he mused to himself. *God, no one does it like you!!*

Throwing her purse strap over her sleek shoulder, Marjorie looked at the Reverend and said, "Today is my day of sacrificial offering. There is no Abraham or Isaac, but the sacrifice is money and I'm going to purchase your suit today. Because ... the Lord has ordered me to do so. Reverend Reeves, you're such a true man of God."

The Reverend would not have taken so kindly to the offering if he were privy to Marjorie's darkness. But he didn't know, so he said, "Glory...Praise the Lord. He's an on time God!" Then he and Marjorie began to march through the busy mall towards their destination.

The Reverend had blessings and plots severely mixed up. He now looked at Marjorie as if God had blessed him with a sugar mama. *There was that entitlement again.* Now in his life there was such a huge role for Marjorie to take part in.

Little did he know, the money being spent that day was just a slice of the fortune she had been cuffing from the church over the years. Her secret was safe, for now.

Marjorie was as sharp as a tack. She was definitely on top of her game. Her husband found out the hard way, after she learned of his litany of infidelities. Especially the affair he was having with a young Instagram model name Monae—*French for money.*

Reverend Reeves didn't know that Marjorie possessed fatal attraction syndrome, and her feelings were not to be toyed with. Paying a hitman to take her husband out, no one knew that Marjorie was responsible for his death. Not even the police. *Yet!*

Chapter 2

While Reverend Reeves and Marjorie were getting a bit more acquainted and splurging at the mall, at Jubilee Baptist Church, choir rehearsal was in session. Keith Bradely, the recently anointed choir director, was getting the choir ready to perform for the 4,300 member congregation.

He knew that Reverend Reeves wouldn't settle for less when it came to uplifting the church, and when it came to that spiritual music. Deep down inside, Keith knew that eighty percent of the church came for the musical performances and he was destined to put on an electrifying concert.

Killer performances kept people coming back. What Reverend Reeves loved about the choir was that their sensational performances kept the offering baskets full. It was like the offering collections was payment for the performance. The choir could blow, and music always attracted new members to the congregation.

Keith, also known as Key-Key, was light skinned. In height, he was 5-feet tall exactly, and weighed about 130, no more. Keith was also gay and always stayed dressed to the max. Not only did he look feminine, but his movements were very much female like. He complained about every little thing that the choir didn't do perfect as if he was Mozart, or some large producer killing it in the music business. Keith was only 26 years old.

Rita, one of the main leaders of the choir, was singing a part of Mary-Mary's song *"It's The God in Me"* until she was abruptly cut off by Keith. Immediately the music stopped.

Snapping his fingers from side to side in the air, "Wait … a … minute … now," Keith further blurted out. "That's scary-scary, not Mary-Mary!"

The rest of the choir looked on as they did all they could not to laugh. Rita was a fantastic singer. Her voice was a 100 times better than her looks. Rita was darkest of all midnights when it came to her complexion. She had very short hair, but she hid it with a pretty weave. Still though, you could see the tracks and glue of the weave on her scalp. You could tell that the 256 pound full figured woman was very much heated, because she was old enough to be Keith's mother, and she knew that she could sing.

"What's the hold up now?" she inquired of Keith as she put her hand on her hip and shifted her weight to one leg. "I sang that just like Mary-Mary!"

"No … you didn't, *boo-boo*," Keith shot back in a sassy tone. "I'm the only director on this train, Miss Thang."

Reverend Reeves' cousin Lawrence, who played the drums wasn't a fan of Keith at all. He was tired of his power trip too.

"Look here, Keith, Key-Key—or whatever you want

to be called. That sounded good. We done been over this song for the last two hours," Lawrence stated in frustration as he eyed Keith through his glasses. "You act as if we're performing at the Gospel Music Awards or something. Shiii..." He caught himself as he was about to curse. "I got thangs to do this here evening."

Lawrence had turned it around it after being wrote off by society. See...before giving his life to the Lord, he'd been a bank robber, and had made his way to the FBI's most wanted list. While incarcerated, he joined the ministry, and upon release he joined Jubilee Baptist.

At 5-foot-6, Lawrence was cut in muscles, to be 42 years old, and possessed a young soul. At that moment he wanted to be on Keith's ass. He'd about had enough of Keith's egotistical ass.

Leaning over and whispering in Lawrence's ear, his running buddy Charles who played the guitar, calmed Lawrence down.

"Let it go, Lawrence. His day is coming. Let's just get this over with, so we can go. We doing this for Earl, not him."

Charles was looked at also by Reverend Reeves as part of the family. In height, Charles was about 6'1". Both he and Lawrence was a cocoa complexion and average weight. They were true ride or die partners. Little did Keith know, neither liked him at all due to his feminine ways and they wanted him out of the choir. It was only one thing that came between them and beating Keith down. It was the Reverend's dirty laundry that Keith was privy too.

Keith's sister Queenie, who was a beautiful red-bone

and 36 years old, was the Reverend's mistress. Also, Reverend Reeves had his hand in a lot of ungodly things no community leader would partake in. Guess the saying is true—no one is perfect. Being a Reverend though, he knew better.

"You just run dem sticks and let me run this choir," Keith replied as he moved his head back and forth chicken-neck style. "I gots this here." He then turned back towards Rita and the choir. "Let's take this from the top again yall!"

As the choir began to sing and clap, Lawrence, Charles, and the rest of the musicians cranked up the tunes. For some reason it now sounded better to Keith. While he orchestrated the choir, he bopped to the music shaking himself like a chick. Keith was out of pocket as far as his character in the church and he didn't care at all. Keith was destined to run the choir his way and he planned to do just that. Keith knew that he held the trump card. And if Reverend Reeves got out of line Keith would play it to the max.

While the choir was finding its groove, Keith continued to bop and orchestrate.

As Lawrence played the drums with perfection, Charles was playing the heck out that guitar. Both of them eyed Keith as he continued to direct to the fullest. Lawrence and Charles both was on the same page in their conscience. Mentally plotting on getting rid of Keith, no matter how Reverend Reeves felt about it, or the consequences of their actions for that matter.

Keith must've felt the vibes because he looked at both Lawrence and Charles and then rolled his eyes.

$ $ $

Riding through North Durham down Alston Avenue, Queenie cruised in her black fully equipped Hyundai Sonata.

The first thing her parents saw when Queenie escaped the womb were her delicious dimples and her huge green eyes. Immediately they named her something royal. By the time she was walking, there were plans for her to enter pageants. That lasted for a while, then Queenie reasoned, *being Miss USA wasn't the greatest thing in the world.* Especially with a brother trying to be prettier than her.

Being the Reverend's mistress, Queenie's head was in the clouds. She felt like she had it going on because the Reverend showered her with gifts. Queenie was styling and flossing in her new whip. Little did she know, Reverend Reeves got her the car to keep her mouth shut, and it was inexpensive. The Reverend's wife owned three vehicles that ranged from 2016 to 2018 models. She possessed a Jaguar, a BMW, and a Lexus.

To the Reverend, Queenie was just one of his many freak-a-leaks in the church. When it came to Queenie though, for some reason, from time to time, she caused the Reverend's heart to throb. Queenie had strong feeling for him too. Stronger than she could have ever imagined. She grabbed her iPhone 6 off the dash.

"Let me call this sneaky negro," Queenie said to herself as she continued to cruise the busy city. "His ass hasn't called me *allll* damn day."

Approaching the red light at the intersection of Alston Avenue and Geer Street, Queenie eased to a stop behind a line of vehicles who also was waiting for the traffic light to turn green. Quickly going to her contact screen which the Reverend was number one on her list, Queenie pressed the call button with her fresh French tip that possessed a huge diamond ring set in 24K gold.

"Your black ass better answer the phone," she murmured anxiously; she wasn't good with rejection. "Cause…you know that I will come over your damn house in a heartbeat."

Queenie was dead serious too. One thing pageantry didn't erase from her is—she didn't mind getting ghetto. On the Reverend, Queenie would blank out at any given moment, and then—praise the Lord.

Just as the light turned green, he answered. "Hello, sweetness," he sweetly whispered in Queenie's ear as she drove through the skyscraper filled blocks and held the iPhone at the same time.

"Sweetness my ass, Earl," she replied. "Where in the hell have you been? You ain't called me or nothing."

"Baby, baaaaby…calm down," Reverend Reeves insisted. "You know I had to go to the mall to pick up my suit that I had tailored."

"Ohhh, that's right," Queenie replied as she felt a bit stupid at the same time. "I forgot, Earl. You know how I get when I don't hear from you."

"I know."

Queenie did miss the Reverend, but she was more focused on what he could do for her than anything else for that matter. "Did you get me anything, Earl?"

Oh Hell nawh! Reverend Reeves mused to himself. *You know, I'ma need some of that good stuff first.*

Queenie should've known how the Reverend did his business by now. They had been carrying on for more than a year in counting.

"I was pressed for time," he finally stated. "Basically, I was in and out. The mall was packed, Queenie. And you know firsthand how paranoid I can be sometimes."

"Well, I still want those Jimmy Choo pumps, Earl. You know I want to look good from head to toe for you tomorrow during the sermon and the musical performance. You know that I'll be on the front row baby, with a nice short skirt on. I might show you a shot on the low and fuck up your sermon." She then laughed as she continued to drive. "*Lord forgive me.* Where are you anyway, Earl?"

"I'm on my way home, Queenie. Matter of fact, I'm almost there now."

Reverend Reeves was nowhere near his home. On the real, he didn't want to hook up with Queenie that day. He thought she was only in it for the money. Plus, once he would've hooked up with her, it would've been hard to get away from her. That's how good the Reverend was laying that thing down. On top of that, Queenie didn't give a damn about the First Lady. It was all about Queenie's whims and desires.

"So, what up after church tomorrow?" Queenie quickly quizzed. "Can we hook up and do a little something-something??"

Reverend Reeves shot back, "Baby I would but you know every Sunday after church, I spend the evening with the Misses."

Queenie blurted with pout, "So when the fuck am I going to get my time with you, Earl Reeves???"

"Can you cut down on the profanity a bit, Queenie?"

Queenie smiled, because she only cussed when dealing with the Reverend. He didn't get timid, but the strength and power this man effortlessly possessed seemed to subside a bit.

"Okay," she eventually said, still grinning.

"Queenie, Tuesday is the earliest, because I have to swing by my condo and collect my money from Marlo and Nu-Nu," the Reverend revealed. Then he asked, "Is that a good time for you? If not, you know I'll make it up to you."

"Queenie knew when Reverend Reeves made a promise to make something up to her, he did just that. She would begin to go down her list of wants, and make him promise to get it.

"So, Tuesday, I guess you're going to get those Jimmy Choo pumps for me, huh?"

He was frowning because he knew the shoes that Queenie wanted cost every bit of a $1,000, yet he still agreed. "Yeah, baby. You will have those shoes Tuesday That's my word." Reverend Reeves always kept his word.

Reverend Reeves was trying to hurry up and get Queenie off the phone before the requests continued to come in. He knew blackmail played a role in his willingness to provide as much as the joy of seeing her smile did. He didn't care though, so long as he was in charge, and having it his way. It was a situation that he created, and he'd have to ease his way out of.

"Well, I'm about to pull onto my property. And I'll see you tomorrow at church. Lay low, and play your position because I'll be with my wife."

Sucking her teeth, as she listened and took in all that the Reverend had to say, she shot back, "I won't make a scene, Earl. I promise."

"Okay then. I'll see you tomorrow. But, don't forget, Tuesday is definitely our day. Meet over at the condo 1 P.M. sharp. And have something sexy on for me to take off of your fine behind."

"I can't wait to see you, Earl," Queenie cooed, as she mashed the end call button.

Shaking her head as she emphatically blushed, and laid her phone down in the console between the front seats, Queenie felt truly loved by Reverend Reeves.

I was already wearing something sexy for you, Queenie mused. Beneath her designer trench coat, she wore only lace panties by Victoria's Secret that matched her red stilettos perfectly.

Little did she know, the Reverend was on his way over to Marjorie's house.

Chapter 3

The *First Lady* of Jubilee Baptist Church, Mrs. Eva Reeves, sat in the living room of the opulent estate she shared with her husband, which sat on a beautiful land of 22 acres. The scene of the mansion Reverend Reeves had built was a site that you would see in a *Better Homes and Gardens* magazine.

Nestled in the butter soft brown leather sofa, Eva tuned into *The House of Pain* on their 84" Samsung television that was mounted on the wall. The home that they possessed was the state of the art. Living on the outskirts of the city, Eva could see Lake Michie out the big bay window of the living room in their security gated community.

Eva was 5'2" in height and weighed around 145 pounds. Being a cinnamon complexion, her features resembled Angela Basset in a way. Even at 49 years old, Eva was still a perfect 10. Her body would give younger women the vapors, because Eva definitely had it going on. That Saturday evening she was wearing a tan sleeveless shirtdress that she got from Nordstrom, and laughed at Uncle Curtis as he acted a fool on her favorite TV show.

"That man is *off the chain*!!!" Eva laughed and stated

as tears rolled out her beautiful brown eyes.

Eva sat on the couch with one leg propped up under her while the other leg dangled off of the couch displaying her perfect pedicured foot.

As the show came to an end, Eva looked at the blue marble clock mounted just above the television. It was 7:30 P.M.

Earl should've been home by now, she thought to herself, as she got up, and slid her feet into her Gucci slides. *It don't take this long to go and pick up a suit. He know that he needs to come home and get rested up for tomorrow.*

Eva knew how Reverend Reeves used to be back in the days. He was a player in his hey day. Since going to prison and doing five years, slowly he got his life back together. Obtaining his high school diploma, behind the harsh prison walls, Reverend Reeves took time to think of a profession that suited him. By him always being a talker, he enrolled himself in the University of Texas Christian, through a pell grant from the state of Texas. Also, obtaining a Masters degree in Theology, he became a minister. Still, he had a few shortcomings that he kept in the dark from Eva, that she thought he had been redeemed from.

Being friends and lovers from the playgrounds and hallways of elementary, Eva had been by Reverend Reeves' side no matter what. Through thick and thin.

Even though he was a minister, Eva knew that her husband was still made of flesh. Sin was always lurking. Especially for Reverend Reeves.

Eva's thoughts, heart, and prayers was always on and with him. She knew that fame was a power. Eva also knew that the devil could use it towards a Reverend's weakness. Being a woman who also was highly educated at the University of North Carolina Central, Eva also was once caught up in the trife life of drugs in her college years. But she overcame it whole heartedly, by the power of God.

Eva now was truly in her heart sanctified and filled with the Holy Spirit. On the real, to the fullest degree, she took her marital vows very serious and would do anything to keep her husband out of the gates of hell.

Reverend Reeves may've been short on hair, but his sexual wellness wasn't lacking. And Eva wanted her husband at that very moment.

But what Eva loved most was the Reverend's ability to join the ranks of the sophisticated and elite.

Remembering where she last had her cell phone, Eva headed to the kitchen. As she made her way through the cherry oak filled dining room, Eva saw her phone laying in the center of the floor on the island.

Entering the kitchen, that looked as if it could've been on a broadcast cooking show, Eva grabbed her phone. Although Eva possessed several diamond rings

Eva kept it simple. She only wore her wedding band and ring. With her delicate finger, she pulled up her husband's number. As she was about to press call, she heard the Reverend pulling up in the garage.

"About time he came home!" Eva happily stated, having heard him exit the vehicle and slam the door.

The garage door was closing at the same time. Walking over to the door of the kitchen to open it for the Reverend, Eva longed for his companionship. Once she opened the door, Eva saw that Reverend Reeves had his arms and hands full of shopping bags and Chinese food.

Holding open the door, Eva shifted her weight to one leg and put her other hand on her hip. "Earl, you'd better had a reason to be gone this long," she lamented as the Reverend made his way in the house. "Honey, you left here at around 1:15 this evening."

"Reverend Reeves headed towards the dining room. He laid the bags on the huge table that sat eight. Eva was dead on his tracks. Approaching him, Eva looked at her husband with a stoic stare. She felt as if she was being ignored; because the Reverend just kept it moving without even saying *hello*.

"Earl, did you hear me talking to you? I..."

Before Eva could jump down his throat, Reverend Reeves wrapped her in his arms and French kissed her. She was the only woman he kissed like that.

Eva became overwhelmed by the kiss, and just that quick she forgot all about the tongue lashing she was going to put on the Reverend. All Eva could do was embrace her husband, hugging him equally and tight as she melted in passionate ecstasy.

Easing out of the smooch, Reverend Reeves looked into Eva's bright eyes. He wanted to lay her on the dining room table, pull her skirt up, slide her panties off, and long stroke his wife. But, instead of physical loving, the Reverend chose mental love which was also charm in his eyes.

"Have a seat baby," he said smoothly, as he pulled a chair from up under the table for her.

"I bought you something nice that you'll love, *bae*."

Obeying, her husband's wishes, Eva sat down in the plush dining room chair. Flattered, she smiled at the same time. *He's so romantic*! she mused.

Reaching out, Reverend Reeves grabbed a Hect's shopping bag and handed it to his wife. "For you, my beautiful sexy queen. God couldn't have blessed me with such a woman as you. Eva, you're all that God speaks of in the bible as far as you being my rib," he said sofly while looking directly in her eyes.

Once she opened the lid of the box and saw the Jimmy Choo pumps that Queenie wanted, Eva quickly jumped up in excitement and draped her arms once again around her husband. *He is so romantic!*

One thing for sure, Reverend Reeves was a very romantic man when it came to his wife.

Together they'd been through hell and back. Even though he had his ways, Eva was still the Reverend's First Lady, not only in the church, but deep down inside his heart. Even though Reverend Reeves had his dark side of life, he kept it hidden from his wife.

Still though…he couldn't keep his secrets from God.

"Thank you, bae," Eva blurted out. "I love them," she further stated as she slipped her feet out of the slides to try them on.

Little did Eva know, Reverend Reeves didn't spend not one dime on her shoes. He used scripture to obtain them. Reverend Reeves was not only the one with all the sense, Marjorie was slick too. She not only hooked the Reverend up, she got something in return—some hard lovemaking.

Looking at his wife rise up and sashay in her pumps, he felt a sense of guilt. He knew Marjorie's love juice was on the kiss he laid on Eva. He covered that up too with his gold ole soap and cologne. Also, he knew that he needed to be headed to the shower to wash off the sins soiling his flesh.

"I'm gonna go on and get ready for supper, Eva."

Eva was strutting in her Jimmy Choo's and only said, "Okay."

Chapter 4

Out in Strawberry Hills sat the most extravagant condos that anyone could imagine. Tennis courts, club house, and patio decks. It was truly glamorous living. Reverend Reeves owned one of the condos that sat on the second floor overlooking the beautiful development.

Nu-Nu and Marlo occupied the spot. The condo was in deed a nice property that the Reverend owned. You would think that Nu-Nu and Marlo paid the Reverend a lot of rent to live in such a nice place and community. The condos were on Newcastle Drive which sat back in the cut with a perfect view of the Whipporwill Park. The neighborhood consisted of a diverse culture.

From Asian, white, Latino, to African American, it was one big melting pot and money flowed and flowed like the Niagara Falls. In this community everyone was in unity and also minded their business. That's why Reverend Reeves had never put the condo on the market. It was home at the beginning of his ministry.

Once he sure enough blew up, the Reverend and Eva got married and she moved in right away. Being a manager for the city of Durham, Eva worked in City Hall. She also brought a lot into the marriage. With Reverend

Reeves' growing ministry and Eva's six figure paying job, they were able to move out the condo and settle down out in the Treyburn area where blacks rarely resided, and hold onto the condo. That's where he had his nephews Nu-Nu and Marlo move his weight from. All sorts of opiods and exotic weeds to go only with the pure cocaine he was getting from a young dude named Edward Haywood. Most of the clientele lived right in the community. So they didn't have to worry about people wanting credit or causing trouble. And the Reverend was the head of the operation, hiding behind the scenes like the wizard of oz. Everyone thought he was the landlord. He could come by the first of every month just like a landlord, and leave with a heavy bag of money. He would also drop off on that day. And only he and his nephews, whom were 24 and 26, were privy.

It was his greedy money hungry mentality that caused the Reverend to catch the five year bid back in the days. He loved the fact of a come up, and drugs was also the game, that he didn't want no one, especially Eva, to know that he still partook in when he didn't have to.

Under the cathedral style ceiling of the condo Nu-Nu stood on the loft od the second floor and looked down at Marlo as he sat on the blue suede plush love-seat weighing and bagging up the last of the product, which was about 10 ounces of pure white cocaine.

Marlo bobbed his head to one of his many playlists of hip hop music. French Montana's *"Unforgettable"* was booming out of the speakers of the digital Bose system.

"Yo, Marlo, please turn that shit down," Nu-Nu blurted out real smoothly but also like a boss. He was the oldest. "Bruh, you know Uncle Earl don't play that shit. We don't need no heat over here."

Standing in his blue Fendi jeans, Nu-Nu had on a wife beater and was only wearing socks because he was lying across the bed with his lady watching the Saturday night basketball game between Duke and North Carolina. In this situation, Nu-Nu was the level headed one. Marlo was straight up hood, and he didn't give a damn about nothing. Life was all about money, music, tricks, clothes, shoes and getting high. Even though no one ever complained, Nu-Nu wanted quietness.

Looking up at Nu-Nu, Marlo glared as if Nu-Nu was crazy. "Nu-Nu…Nu-Nu," Marlo elaborated. "Go on back in the room with Felita. I'm fixing to get rid of the last of this yayo. Uncle Earl's gonna be over here Tuesday for his scratch," he further stated as he put the big blocks of rock on the black and gray digital scale.

Since little boys, they looked up to their uncle. Being misled in life, Nu-Nu and Marlo thought the lifestyle that Reverend Reeves lived was cool. They only took into consideration the money and fame, not the consequences. Both of them went to church high on weed, just to hear their uncle put his sermons down. It was funny to Nu-Nu and Marlo because they knew the Reverend had another side to him. *God did too!*

With his charcoal colored slender body, Marlo extended his arm and grabbed the remote to the sound system that sat on the round glass coffee table beside the scale. He didn't want to go through it tonight with Nu-Nu. They went through their spats, but one thing for certain, they were down like two flat tires.

Taking a break for a couple minutes, Marlo got up and headed towards the kitchen. "You want a shot of Hen-rock, bruh?" Marlo asked with no shirt on. All he sported was his Cuban link iced out gold chain that hung down to the center of his chest with an iced out 50 caliber Desert Eagle medallion.

His black Gucci jeans was hanging off his butt, even though he had on a leather Gucci belt with the iced out Gucci buckle. To top it all off, Marlo had on the black and white Gucci sneakers setting the tone. Both, he and Nu-Nu could definitely make it rain with the Benjamins. It was all because they were doing the Reverend's dirty work.

"Nah, I'm good, bruh. I'm about to go back in the room with Felita," Nu-Nu replied. "Just keep the music down. Felita was nearly sleep. I'm trying to creep out later on. Save me four of them things, because at about

12:15 I got a score over in Carver Pond, and it's a come up too."

From the kitchen, as he was getting ice, Marlo yelled, "You know where it be at."

"Cool, I'm out," Nu-Nu replied. "You need to check out the game. It's off the hook."

"*Man, later for that game*," Marlo stated under his breath, as he entered the living room with a glass of Henessey on ice. "*I am the game*."

Nu-Nu shook his head as he looked at Marlo sit back down on the love seat, portraying as if he was Scarface or some drug lord in the Andes.

"The only thing I want to see is this shit gone so Uncle Earl can hit us off again Tuesday," Marlo expl-ained as he sat the glass of liquor on the table.

There was a knock at the door. Nu-Nu waited to see who it was before stepping off. Reaching under the sofa for his heat, Marlo quickly got it, got up, and headed towards the heavy knocking. "Who in the hell is it?" Marlo asked, slowly approaching the door to look through the peep-hole.

"It's me, nep, …! Ole Pokey," the voice said back through the cedar wood door.

Holding the silver weapon, a sense of relief came over Marlo as he saw Pokey through the peep-hole.

Putting the pistol in his waistband, Marlo took the dead-bolt off and allowed Pokey in while cussing him out.

"Man, why you didn't ring the doorbell?? You know, knocking all loud and shit like the vice."

Pokey was Reverend Reeves' handyman. As far as cars and properties, he did all of the Reverend's work for the low-low. Pokey grew up with Reverend Reeves back in the hood when the Reverend was down and out. No matter what Pokey always hung tight with the Reverend. Pokey knew that one day his buddy would strike it big. The two friends were only a year apart, but worlds apart when it came to perspective. Pokey was robbed of success when he allowed cocaine to cripple his life. That's how the Reverend always paid Pokey.

For the last couple of days, he'd been on a spree. Now that there was no more coke to do, Pokey was on "E" and needed a wake-up. It was odd though, because he never came by the spot at this time of the night.

"Marlo, throw me an eight-ball," the tall scary looking man requested. "You know I'm good for it."

Standing in the doorsill, Marlo stood and looked at Pokey. In height, Pokey was about 6'1" and weighed every bit of a buck-fitty. His head was balled on top and peasy on the sides, and looked like it was too big for his body. He was a dark brown complexion and he always wore a blue Dickies one-piece work suit and some ran over brown Timberland boots that was stained up from all the different jobs he did. Pokey had a full gray beard. If he took a bath and groomed himself, he could be a handsome man.

His work ethic was on point and he would've made any woman happy. But, Pokey always blew his money on coke. The Reverend only moved power through Nu-Nu and Marlo. What he didn't know was, Marlo had begun to cook the coke behind the Reverend's back, turning his uncle's longtime chum out in the process.

Nu-Nu headed back to his bedroom after he seen that it was Pokey. Marlo gave Pokey a stern look as Nu-Nu closed the door behind him. No one was supposed to know that he'd been giving Pokey the potent substance.

One thing for sure is that Reverend Reeves wanted no parts of the crack game. That type of business brought a different mentality to the people. The customers that the Reverend had were doctors, lawyers, and other people with high status in society. Some were even in politics. He even had a few customers that were preachers. It was all about the power and love of money.

"Pokey…you can't let Nu-Nu know about the crack I've been giving you, and selling through you," Marlo stated, making his way back to the love seat. "Unc, thinks you been grabbing powder," he added.

"Shiiit, Marlo," Pokey replied as he watched Marlo place the pistol back in its hiding place. "I ain't said a word to nobody."

"Your ass ain't got to say shit. Look at you. That's saying a lot," Marlo shot back. "I'ma give you some of this powder, but you got to slow your roll."

Marlo looked at Pokey as if he was also an uncle. Anytime that he needed something done, Pokey was the go-to man. Reaching for one of the plastic sandwich bags that sat in a box, also on the table, Marlo began to sniff around in the air.

"Pokey, you need to hit that water too. You stink."

"You'sa damn lie," Pokey replied in an embarrassed tone as he watched Marlo put some coke in a bag.

Marlo was suddenly overcome by the urge to get on Pokey. Only because he knew he was Pokey's god in a way. "When's the last time you took that work suit off? I know you done farted in that bitch a hundred time."

Reverend Reeves would've slapped Marlo for handling Pokey in such a manner. That was his buddy from the sandbox, no matter what.

Getting up off the sofa, Marlo handed Pokey the bag, and escorted him to the door. "For real, don't let unc know. And don't say shit to my brother."

"Nephew, you know I won't. It's between us," Pokey shot back as Marlo opened the door. "When you gonna get you a good girl and settle down, like yo brother?"

"When I meet the right one," Marlo replied, shutting the door.

Pokey smiled as he strolled to his vehicle. From the window, Marlo watched the beat-up '84 brown Dodge work van take off.

Pokey pulled off through the parking lot towards the exit of the condos. After making a left on Newcaslte

Drive, a head popped up in the back of the van where the tools were.

"Did you make the *buy*?" Officer Jamie Green asked.

Pokey had been out in Braggtown projects, in his van, getting high with a trick. Being careless, he let an undercover cop run down on him as he was smoking crack with a trick, in exchange for oral pleasure. Pokey didn't want to go to jail, he had never been in trouble, so he agreed to do anything to prevent the arrest.

Officer Jamie Green was a short stocky white dude who was destined to make rank in the department. After pressure from a tough interrogation, Pokey vowed to give his connect up. Like a disloyal bitch, Pokey mentioned the condos, but no names, instead of falling on the sword he'd left sticking up.

Now, not only was the condo hot, but the Reverend could also feel the domino effect. Because of Pokey, an investigation was on the horizon. But for some reason, Marlo didn't request any money. The buy money was still in Pokey's pocket.

All Pokey did was escape a jail cell. He didn't know that the wrath of the Reverend was a long ways from the scripture of turning the other cheek.

Chapter 5

"*Everything that happened to me, that was God, God did it!*" sang Rita, with veins raising on her neck.

The choir replied, "*God did it...oh yes he...did it!*"

It was a beautiful Sunday morning and Jubilee Baptist Church was very much alive. All 4,300 members of various shades and creeds were on their feet, on the floor, and the mezzanine, as Rita stood in the burgundy robe holding the microphone. She moved the church in spirit as she blew the song "God Did It" while the choir backed her up and swayed from side to side in their robes as well.

Lawrence, Charles and the rest of the musicians was on point with the music, while Keith stood and directed with his hair braided in a style like Alicia Keys.

The outfit he wore was something Liberace would have captivated the masses with in his day. Keith would not be denied that day.

Reverend Reeves and the First lady sat in the pulpit surrounded by his deacons as if was the second black president of the United States.

Reverend Reeves was not only into the song with joy but he was full of jubilee because he had a clear view of Marjorie and the ushers taking up the offering.

Twenty big bamboo baskets circulated throughout the church from the floor to the mezzanine. The congergation gave a nice portion of the wages they've earned from their jobs, retirement, SSI, and public assistance checks.

As Rita and the choir lit up the church with that joyous sound, the congregation kept giving and giving.

Watching the ushers work the aisles, Marjorie danced and clapped, dressed in a blue long sleeved dress that had glitter flakes throughout it by Versace. Not only was the Reverend happy, but so was Marjorie. She knew out of all the money baskets, her cut was definitely coming. As if she was full of the spirit, Marjorie moved about from side to side with her hands raised high as if she was Shirley Caesar.

Once the ushers took up all of the money, quickly they made their way back to stand in front of the pulpit. Reverend Reeves sat and watched all twenty ushers as they stood side by side with Marjorie in the middle and baskets in the air to show their seize.

Quickly, Reverend Reeves stood with his wife and all the Deacons. Observing all the baskets that were overflowing with money and tithing envelopes, he raised his hands as in thanks to God, which was also the signal for Keith to have the choir close out.

With a keen eye, Reverend Reeves turned his gaze to Marjorie letting her know to proceed along with the ushers to the Trustee's office, where the baskets would be counted.

As the choir carried out Keith's orders, and the musicians softly continued with the music, everyone in the pulpit took a seat except Reverend Reeves. The congregation continued to stand, shout and dance up and down the aisles.

To further electrify the congregation, the Reverend stood in his black suit with glowing gold pinstripes. In his sermon tone, mic in hand, he shouted as the music stopped, "*Who did it? Congregation, who did it?*"

Then as he hummed, the Reverend pointed to the people in the mezzanine –"*Who did it?*"

"*God did it!*" they all responded in unison, and with conviction. Thousands could be heard.

"*Won't he do it?*" Reverend Reeves continued. "*Won't he do it?*" Then he began to stir up the crowd. "Some of you was on drugs, some were alcoholics, and a few of you chose the dark side. But...look at you now...*Won't he do it*?"

"*Yeeessssss!*" the congregation shouted back.

"I said—*won't he do it?*"

Some of the congregation rapidly shouted, while others cried and raised their hands to the sky. The dancing and running of the aisles resumed as well.

Reverend Reeves was still standing and observing from his vantage point. He realized that a lot of his members were really redeemed from their shortcomings, just as he had been.

Just as King Saul in the bible had, Reverend Reeves was doing as he wanted to do. Deep down inside, he knew that he was being disobedient. But even though the Reverend knew all of this, he continued to serve God which was best suited for his extravagant lifestyle.

Chapter 6

Detective Ewing was an older pudgy white man in his early fifties, and the Lieutenant of the Durham Police narcotics squad. Lt. Ewing was sipping on a hot cup of cappuccino as he sat at his desk reading the crime section of the local newspaper on a sort of busy day, when he peeped Officer Green coming towards his office.

What is he doing here on his day off? the Lt. wondered while peeking over the paper.

Seeing Green chat with a couple of the other lawmen as he passed through the stationhouse, Lt. Ewing sat the paper down.

As the Officer rapped on the door, the Lieutenant invited him in. "It's Sunday, why aren't you enjoying you day off?"

Officer Green replied, "Remember that guy that I picked up in the Braggtown projects, who was in the van smoking crack with the streetwalker?"

Having thought about the past incident, the Lt. extended his hand saying, "Have a seat, refresh my memory."

"Well, you had given us foot patrol detail, and I walked up on his van while the woman was performing oral on him while he smoked. He had an eight-ball of crack on him."

"Okay, I do recall," the Lt. lamented now searching his desk for the incident report. "Here it is, Richard Jones, right?"

"Yeah, he goes by Pokey in the streets," Officer Green quickly added as he watched the Lt. rub his bald head in small circles. "Okay, we didn't charge him because he agreed to inform," the Lt. added leaning back in his black leather office chair.

"That is correct, sir."

Being the superior officer, Lt. Ewing relinquished an expression of *this better be good.* Sitting up in his chair, and giving Officer Green a stern look, he said, "I'm listening."

Giving Lieutenant Ewing the full rundown, Green went on saying, "Of course when I crept up on Richard Jones and arrested him, he cried like a bitch. Anyway, he started telling me about some guy named Marlo."

"Does this Marlo guy seem to be a heavy hitter?" Lt. Ewing asked.

"I'm getting to that part," Officer Green explained. "Anyway...what he told me was convincing, so I gave him a try. I gave him a one shot deal and one shot only. He told me about this spot over Strawberry Hills."

"Strawberry Hills?" Lt. Ewing said in an astonished tone. "Only big shots live out there in those condos. Not no crack-heads or dealers. So, he was singing more than Usher. That's how I found out his street name."

"Okay, okay!" Lt. Ewing was liking what he was hearing. "Anything else, Green?"

"Well, I told the trick to take a walk and wrote Pokey a bogus citation. Also, I gave him a card. I told him that he'd better call me in two hours and I will have the buy money."

With an inquiring mind, Lt. Ewing asked, "Did he call you yet?"

"And..., he took me to the spot."

"Did he make the buy???" the Lt. asked with an eager look in his eyes.

"Yes, he did, Lt. I rode in the back of the van, and watched him enter the spot and exit the spot. Pokey came through."

"So what's the hold up with the bust? You tested it and everything, I know."

"It was pure," Green replied. "The purest that this city has seen in a long time."

"How pure was it?" the Lt. asked with a frown because of the danger the potent product presented.

"Ninety-eight percent pure...I can't believe no one has overdosed or even died."

"Green, try to buy an ounce of it. That will tell you if it's a big supply of it. Start an indictment go higher and higher, with the buys. Build a case."

"Lt, I need for you to listen to the twist in current events of this case."

In a deep suspense, Lt. Ewing looked at Officer Green. For a minute or two, he was lost in the sauce.

"Okay, what's the twist?" he asked, giving officer Green his attention now to the fullest.

"Well, I ran the address of the condo. The name Marlo is nowhere on the deed."

"Whose name is on the deed?"

"You're right, it's big time people who live out there," Officer Green relayed. "The condo is owned by Reverend Earl Reeves, who is the Reverend of the Jubilee Baptist Church on Roxboro Road."

The Lieutenant's eyes lit up in suspense. "Do you think the Reverend is involved in any way?" he asked.

Officer Green replied, "It's something going on because this so called Marlo lives in this expensive neighborhood and has no job."

"So do you think that we need to put Reverend Reeves in the indictment?" the Lt. asked in disbelief.

"The finger points to him as well, because with cocaine this pure, only someone with money and connectoins can supply this guy. The condo is in his name also." Then in a delish tone, Green laid a blow with, "Marlo's last name is Reeves. He's the Reverend's nephew! His goddamn nephew. He has to know!"

Lt. Ewing smiled like a sneaky possum with Green's revelation reverberating in his 55-year old mind. He got his rocks off using his authority to get to the top. He wanted to be Captain, and Green dreamed of becoming sergeant one day. And that day had come faster than they could've ever imagined. Two ambitious cops scheming…

Now that this investigation was pointing towards a big positive figure in the community, it was definitely news for the media, which would get the promotions that Green and Ewing so craved. That is, if the indictment was in fact successful.

Chapter 6

When Reverend Reeves finally opened the doors of the church, people flowed full of happiness and uplifted in spirit. While some stood outside conversing, others hurried to their vehicles. Still inside the church, Lawrence saw Rita congregating with members of the choir. He took the alone time to reflect on his day and the days ahead. After Rita's chat was over, Lawrence approached Rita and invited her out to dinner at the Golden Corral.

Rita was once a beautiful woman. It wasn't until she caught her man in her bed with another woman that she lost her way. Rita's man was her everything, and without him she was empty. Women were always fawning over him, so she had to do a little extra to keep him happy. Even that proved to be moot.

Quickly, she fell into a state of depression, which led to unnecessary eating habits, and she blew up. Rita went from an attractive 165 to a portly 256, almost overnight. Lawrence could still see beauty in her. Looking past the paunch, and the triple D's, he saw raven eyes that were on a slant; and cute lips he wouldn't have mind kissing.

Over the chatter of families, rambunctious kids, and folk bum-rushing the buffet, Lawrence and Rita were seated at a table for two by a short white waitress with dirty blonde hair.

Rita thought the waitress could be a sophomore in college. She introduced herself as if she was not expecting Lawrence and Rita to tip her on their way out. With menus and silverware in hand, the waitress laced the brown glossy wood table for two, before stating in a nonchalant tone, "My name is Tina, and I'll be your server today." She talked fast and rolled her eyes with each word. "What kind of beverage would you like to drink?"

Together, Lawrence and Rita replied, "Sweet Tea, please."

Quickly, as the waitress made her way to the beverage station, Rita gave her a heard stare and said, "Lawrence, I was about to lose my religion up in here."

"I saw it all over your face," Lawrence replied, as he reached over and caressed Rita's hand to ease the tension.

Rita was about to keep their conversation rolling, when the waitress returned and interrupted them with their drinks.

"Here's your tea," she blurted out in an unpleasant manner, sat their teas down hard, and stormed off.

As the waitress walked away, Rita looked at her pony-tail as it bounced. She could've snatched if off of her damn head.

"Be nice," Lawrence quickly suggested, and massage Rita's puffy hand. "What would Jesus do?"

"I'm not trying to hear all that, Lawrence," Rita stated as she shook her head. "Keith already got me pissed. *Been hot with him since rehearsal Saturday.*"

"Yeah, I'm about sick of him too. Earl has just done let him take over. How did he take Doug's director position anyway?" Lawrence inquired, as he released his grasp and then reached for his glass of tea.

"That's what we're all trying to figure out. It's just too much dealing with Keith. Either *this note ain't right*, or *it's the musicians*."

"And he ain't singing or playing nothing at all," Lawrence interjected. "Keith just want to stand up in the spotlight and try to catch on the low. All of that bopping and sashaying mess he be doing, I know Earl be seeing it too. Keith is out of pocket."

"He definitely is. To be honest, Lawrence, I'm about burned out on Keith. Pastor Fisher already wants me to come sing at his church, *Spirit of Joy Baptist.* Honestly, I'm about ready to take him up on his offer."

Rita didn't really want to leave Jubilee Baptist, because Reverend Reeves ranked high as far as leadership within the community churches, and refused to let Rita's insecurities with her weight hinder her potential as a gospel singing star.

Quickly, Lawrence sat his glass down on the table, and said in disbelief, "Rita, don't do that. You were in the choir first. We can't afford to lose someone as talented as you. Earl will have a fit! Trust me, he knows he has a star on his hands."

People began to pay attention to Lawrence and Rita, but Lawrence didn't care, he knew Rita could blow the roof off a church or any tabernacle in any state. With her voice she could give even Patti Labelle a run for her money. Rita could hit every note, and could probably be signed to any of the top gospel record labels if she put her mind to it, and could even cross over into the R&B sector of music. Reverend Reeves was getting a deal on Rita's services because of her love of God and her love for singing.

"Well, he better do something about Keith,"--there was a pause--"Because I'm not going to keep going through the hassle." Tears formed in her saddening eyes. "Lawrence, enough is enough."

Seeing Rita break down, Lawrence felt compelled to have her back. He knew something must be done about Keith. But, he chose to change the topic because they weren't in the place for that.

"Rita, calm down. I'm here for you," Lawrence assured her. "Everything will work out. Just remember, what we do, *we do it for God.* Not Keith." Reaching and corralling Rita's hand again, he added, "Now listen, I brought you out to the restaurant to relax and have a good time, after that awesome performance you gave us today. F--- Keith, babygirl."

Rita laughed at Lawrence's successful attempt to refrain from cussing. "Lawrence, I've been holding my feelings in for a while now. Ever since Keith's been directing, it's been nothing but drama. He's caused not only me, but others in the choir, much pain."

I know, I know...and he will be dealt with. Rita, believe that. I will talk to Earl myself," Lawrence vowed then smiled showing his gold tooth. "That frustration you've got--why don't you got to *Planet Fitness*, and exercise with me. You'll feel much better."

With a surprised look all over her face, Rita couldn't believe that Lawrence invited her to the gym with him. It was something that she often thought about.

Lawrence was so muscular and fit, and had very little body fat. Rita had noticed that the moment Lawrence first walked into Jubilee Baptist. She could also tell his body was built on a weight pit at a penitentiary. Rita knew this, because on occasions she could browse through websites for prison pen-pals, and see the guys flaunting their physiques. She believed that prisoners needed friends, and even lovers too. But she never got the courage up to write any of those beautiful brothers craving a little attention.

Lawrence was looking at her as if he could read her mind, and flexed a little.

Rita lit up with joy. "Yes, I'll work out with you. Just don't hurt me, Lawrence."

"Well, we got a date! Tuesday when I get off of work," Lawrence said, smiling. "I'll pick ya up at four."

Rita put both hands over her mouth. She was submerged in awe. *Lawrence wants to exercise with me???* This was new ground, and Rita was ready to break it. *Could sex be next???* she wondered.

"Come on, let's get out here, and get our grub on. I'm hungrier than a hostage," said Lawrence, now getting up and holding on to Rita's hand.

Rita was experiencing nervousness and elation, and felt that all this was too good to be true, in such a short period of time.

Going with the flow, Rita allowed Lawrence to lead her towards the many buffets of varying foods. It was good to know that a man could still find her attractive and interesting.

"You alright, Lawrence."

"You is too, Rita," Lawrence said cooly.

Chapter 7

That night out on Guess Road in the luxurious Crystal Pine development, Marjorie sat in the dining room of her sprawling 4-bedroom split level brick home. She had stacks in order ranging from $100 bills to singles.

Over a two piece chicken dinner from KFC, this was her normal routine. Marjorie hadn't used her kitchen much since her husband's unsolved murder. KFC had become her form of sustenance. With buttermilk biscuits beside the chicken, Marjorie tallied her take of the Jubilee Baptist Church's offering.

For the last five years, ever since she'd been elected Chief of Offering collection, Marjorie had grossed no less than $1,200 tax free each Sunday.

If the church's accountant questioned her, Marjorie would simply say, –"*It's not a set figure to look for. The congregation gave what they could.*" And no one would question it, because according to her, she came from money. And, she did have the life insurance money, along with the rest of her husband's assets.

As she continued to fondle through the big face bills, Marjorie couldn't help but smile and think about the deep penetration Reverend Reeves had laid on her the day before. Her husband, when he was alive and kicking, had never gave up it like that man. He sexed Marjorie down with absolutely no insufficiencies.

Marjorie was at a vulnerable state in life, which is what led her to sneak thieving the very people who would have given her their last. It wasn't about the money though, it was the thrill of possibly getting caught or looking the accountant square in the eye and lying to conceal her sins. And just that fast, the Reverend filled a void. Yet, there were no immediate plans to retire from stealing from the offering, or stealing from the First Lady of Jubilee Baptist.

At church services earlier that day, Reverend Reeves didn't know that Marjorie was fantasizing that it was she who was sitting beside him instead of Eva Reeves. His charisma, style, smarts, looks and the sermons had always turned Marjorie on. Even while her husband was alive. She just honored their vows in God's eyes, and held her yearning in. My how things had changed.

Now that she no longer had to fantasize, and things had materialized, she intended to see more of the Reverend. And, whenever she wanted to. When it came to lovemaking, her body was a sacred temple. ...*The Reverend's temple*. And he had better cherish it.

The Reverend didn't know he'd lit a candle that wouldn't be easy to blow out. Obsession was now flowing through Marjorie's veins. A fatal attraction was on the horizon. In his eyes, that Saturday afternoon rump was just a fling. On the other hand, Marjorie knew no limits, no matter who got hurt, as long as the flame continued to flicker.

She bit down into her crispy drumstick, smiling like she'd never smiled before. Beneath the huge table she was sitting at, her thighs were clinched so tightly, she burst out into laughter. "You ain't got nothing on my Reverend, *Mister Kentucky Fried Chicken.*"

Chapter 8

It was a beautiful Monday evening. Keith had just got off of work. *Sparkle's Hair Salon* was his day job. And he had Queenie to thank for that as well. He began his career styling hair by getting creative with Queenie's beautiful hair when he was fourteen. By the time he was finishing up high school, he was one of the hottest stylist to split a wig. Wasn't a damn thing anyone could tell Keith.

"Queenie, Queenie ...I know you hear me calling you girllll!" he blurted out as he strutted down the hallway where family portraits decorated the walls.

Queenie and Keith were not just super tight siblings, they also were roommates in the Pepper Tree Townhouse community, out in the Willowdale shopping center area. The neighborhood was very much upscale, most of the residents of the townhouse getaway were college students at Duke, the University of North Carolina, N.C. Central, and North Carolina State. So they fit right in.

The area was very much alive with the LGBTQ community, to the Black social justice activists. Ethnicity, sexuality, or political party was not a problem. It was a very safe living environment.

Keith saw the sliding glass door open and figured Queenie was out on the patio. The cedar wood deck was furnished to the max.

"*Queenie...girl,*" Keith cooed elaborately, as he headed towards the opening. Queenie's head was buried in a book. "Didn't you hear me calling you? I saw your car…so I knew you were here," said Keith as he sat in the rust style castor-iron chair, with a silk flower print beige cushion. He snapped his fingers the way a diva would. "*Shiiiit*, I was about to do some *karate* up in this bitch."

Queenie didn't respond because the book she was reading had her undivided attention.

Keith saw that he couldn't get his sister's eyes to leave the pages, so he did what he does best…signify.

"Girl …what are you reading that got your attention all wrapped the fuck up, sis?" he asked, scooting back in the chair. He crossed one leg over the other, just as Queenie looked up to see her brother in some shorts that were shorter than the one hugging her juicy ass and hips. "Earl has never had you in a trance like that."

Queenie smiled at her brother, then said, "This book *Nothing Is Sacred* is off the hook. I got to tell my girlfriends about this book. They've got to get this."

"Well…tell me, so I can get it. Who is it by?"

"Keith, it's by BOOG DENIRO. And you cannot read it. You have to get your own. Because I'm going to read and read it over and over. Now go on, Keith."

"Hold up, *Miss Thang*. Don't try to get all jazzy now," Keith snapped back quickly. He hated being dismissed. "I was just checking up on your *Indian looking ass*. Don't make me read you out here."

Queenie mimicked Keith's *sister-girl* gesticulation. He had it down better than Queenie. He then said, "I got something to talk to you about anyway. It's been eating at my bones since Saturday. And, that shit ain't flying!"

Neighbors were out on their decks, while others were out walking their dogs. Keith didn't care at all. The more attention, the more he believed he was getting his point across. Being loud was his way of life. His voice carried like *Medea's*.

"What is it, Keith?" Queenie asked, laying her book down on her lap. "Pleeeease, make it quick."

Rolling his eyes at Queenie, Keith began with, "Look, I'm about tired of Rita's big ass up in the choir trying to tell me how to run my show."

He let that settle in on Queenie, and she said, "Okay?"

"I need for you to holler at Earl. Because, I want her out of the sanctuary."

Queenie giggled at her brother because he was very dramatic. Keith would turn an ant-hill into a mountain, if things didn't go his way.

Keith then added, "And Lawrence can get the hell on too, since he wants to be her knight in shining armor."

"Earl's not going for that. Rita is his best singer, and has been for years. So that definitely ain't going down. Then, you talking about Lawrence. Not only is he Earl's family, but he's a dangerous man," she warned her brother before getting back to her book. "And who would replace Rita anyway???"

"Dangerous???"

"Yes, that is what I said."

"I'm dangerous," Keith replied, then added, "Oooh, don't worry about all of that. I got somebody."

"Oh really?" Queenie said, with her eyebrows on fleek. She then did this little sniggle thing that made Keith irate.

"Honey, it's already in the oven and done! I just started doing her hair! And her ass can sang! She sounds like Yolanda Adams. You just talk to Earl…or I will."

Queenie didn't want to get caught up in the middle of the situation. Keith was her brother, and Earl was her man. It was either blood, or the glamorous life. And Keith was hell bent on creating a major problem.

Chapter 9

Later that evening, Reverend Reeves was out and about in Wellons Village Shopping Center, which was located over in the hood. The Reverend had spent his first fifteen years in that area of Durham.

Any name brand item, when it came to clothes, shoes or accessories, the Reverend knew exactly where to go. *True Finesse!* He was there on behalf of Queenie.

A friend from middle school, a Korean fellow by the name of Han, would also hook the Reverend up.

Han was very short, about 4-foot-11. He put you in the mind, when it came to resemblance, of Jackie Chan. So called ballers and divas shopped at his store for the latest fashion. It was hard to tell Han's black market inventory for the authentic design. From his wife down to his grandchildren, Han and his family were employed at True Finesse.

The hottest and newest rap and pop music could be heard playing in the store. With a desire to fit in, Reverend Reeves dressed down. He knew Wellons Village not only attracted shoppers, but it also brought out the stickup kids. So he wore a gray short sleeve shirt and some Levis blue 501 button fly jeans, with some gray suede Wallaby's. He left all his jewelry home, and wore a Seiko just to keep time. The watch was a gift one of the members gave him from a past Pastor's Anniversary celebration.

Walking up the sidewalk, from the corner of his eye, he could she someone being shook down by two goons, and was not only glad to have reached Han's store, but also that he hadn't worn his jewelry.

Inside, as Future's *"Comas"* played, the Reverend peeked out the window to see if the robbery was over. There was a part of him that wanted to dial 911. But he wasn't the only witness. The store was packed. People were dancing and chatting while they shopped. Wall to wall, rack to rack, price tags dangled from items. A two women to one man ratio was also obvious to the Reverend. And his eyes roamed. He couldn't help himself. Queenie's ass wasn't as big as K. Michelle's, but it had the same shape. But Queenie nor Eva would never dress like the women in Han's were dressed. Ass was hanging out the bottom of their shorts and miniskirts. And ole Earl was loving it, and kind of missed that part of his old life. *The fast, the flashy.*

Han and some of his family members watched every move their consumers made. They walked the aisles slowly and quickly, protecting their interests while pretending to assist people.

Reverend Reeves looked around, and noticed Han assisting a short and thick redbone in tight jeans. He didn't leave her side until she was at the counter.

His wife rang the woman's stuff up, and Han walked off looking to get someone else to run it up. That's when he took notice of his longtime friend. He laughed in this friendly Asian way as he approached the Reverend. "Looka who come to see me," he said extending his hand for the Reverend's. "It's my friend, Earl Reeves. Or should I just call you *Reverend?*"

Han was laughing because no matter how well the Reverend was doing or how much change he made in his life, he would always remember him for being wild. Never in a thousand years would Han have imagined his buddy - not only giving his life to God - but preaching the word at his own church too. It was too good to be true.

"My man, Han," the Reverend replied, glad to see an old friend doing good. "I'm here for some shoes."

First Han embraced the Reverend, then said, "So it is shoes that bring you to the Village with us po' people."

Even though Han was Korean, being raised in America and growing up in Liberty Square Projects, all Han's homey's and ex-girlfriends were black. But subscribing to rituals, he stayed within his race and culture when he began his family. Everything about him was urban, even his taste in food.

"Shoes; what kind?" asked Han, now getting serious.

"Jimmy Choo. A birthday gift for the misses."

Han giggled again. "No Jimmy Choo, but I got Vera Wang. And I got a good deal for you."

"Look, Han. I'm looking for Jimmy Choo pumps. That's all she talks about."

He was already taking a chance shopping for Queenie in that part of town, so he had to come correct. See Queenie was ghetto, but still fabulous. Men were always liking her pictures on Instagram and Facebook. And the Reverend had no doubts Queenie could have any of those younger guys if she chose to.

"No, no, no," Han replied as he began to walk towards his woman's shoe department. "You want Vera Wang," he reaffirmed, as he continued to walk past the busy shoppers. "All the ladies love Vera Wang!"

Once Han and Reverend Reeves arrived in the woman's shoe department, Han pointed to a mannequin that displayed the shoes that he was speaking so highly of. Two women were there checking out the display.

Reverend Reeves glanced at their faces to see if they were in fact feeling the shoes. To his surprise, they were. He decided purchase three pairs. Red, black, and butter scotch. He couldn't wait to see her face.

Han had given him the homey price too. $300 for three pairs of designer pumps.

Queenie was the last person the Reverend wanted to piss off. She held the fate to his marriage in her hands. And besides, Queenie looked a whole lot better when she was smiling and not frowning.

Chapter 10

Later that evening and near darkness, Marlo pulled up in his chromed out burgundy 2017 Nissan Maxima. He parked in the resident's reserved spaces, in front of their condo. Turning off the ignition, and getting out, he was approached by a woman with a black cocker spaniel on a leash.

As she walked her dog, her nice fudge brown frame definitely was making a statement, in this super tight *Fabletics* outfit. Seeing this new face in the community caused Marlo to hurry and got out of his car. He couldn't help but see the rump-shaker that this woman possessed, as he stood by his car, with the door still ajar.

He said, "*Daaaaamn*," smoothly as she passed by him. "Miss, you got it going on!" Marlo didn't give a damn, he spoke his mind, and his second-mind.

Marlo's comment made the woman blush and say, "Thank you," as she stopped, unable to conceal the look of elation on her face. "My name is Tracey, not *Miss*, and I just moved out here two weeks ago. You live out here?"

Marlo replied, "Yeah, right here." He pointed to his doorway which they were only a few feet from. "I been living out here for about three years now."

As Tracey checked Marlo out, from head to toe, she noticed that he was handsome and quite flashy. Marlo was sporting a gray and white sweatsuit by New Balance. On his feet were a pair of gray 1500 NB's. As for his neck, wrist and hands, Marlo's jewelry game was batting a thousand. He had just made a run to drop off the last of the product, so he and Nu-Nu would be ready for their Uncle's arrival the next day. But having come across this cutie, Marlo couldn't have come back at a better time. Pictures of sexing her down were flashing through Marlo's creative mind as they exchanged words. It was just the dog in him.

"Tracey, I'm Marlo. Welcome to Strawberry Hills. You moved to the best spot in town. Because of *me*!"

"You live alone?" she quizzed, with one brow raised. "The rent must be sky-high. What kind of job you got?"

Daaaaamn! You nosey as hell! Marlo thought while still holding a smile on his face. "Ahh, nah, me and my cousin share space." He quickly added a lie: "We actually own the place. An inheritance from the family."

"Ohh, a trust fund baby," Tracey stated as she tried to keep her dog still at the same time.

Marlo asked her what she did for a living and Tracey said, "I work at a bank Chapel Hill. It pays the bills."

Marlo then came on strong, "Do you have anyone special in your life? I want a shot at the title, if not."

"Without knowing anything about me, Marlo?" Before he could say anything, Tracey said, "I'm single.

No one special in my life. Negros are shiesty these days, so I'm in no rush to commit to anyone."

"I hear that. But you can't hold all men accountable for the negligence of one. Plus, you deserve happiness."

As she continued to hold the dog by the leash, Tracey put her other hand on her hip, and said, "True, true."

Seeing that dog was not a threat, Marlo got closer to Tracey. "I got some sense. Why don't you let me show you…by allowing me one date. Just one."

"I don't know, Marlo," Tracey stammered, as if her mind wasn't already made up. But she played hard to get, nudged Marlo a bit to put some space back between them, then said, "You're moving a bit quick, ain't you?"

Marlo bent over and patted the dog. Showing his worldly knowledge he said, "Cocker spaniel, right?"

"Yes. I'm surprised you knew. Her name's Gretel."

Marlo looked up, grinning, and returned, "Did that get me a date?"

As he stood back up, Tracey looked into his brown eyes feeling an attraction. His demeanor was bold, he was outspoken and didn't appear to present a threat, so she said, "Sure. Why not??? But you better be who you said you are."

"How about Wednesday? I'm thinking Kyoto's."

"Oh, you're pulling no stops, huh?" Tracey chimed.

Tracey just didn't know Marlo's status in the streets. Because of the Reverend, his bankroll was husky. She had no idea that the money Marlo was about to spend at

Kyoto's was a raindrop in a bucket. Marlo was the rain man.

Kyoto's was an expensive Japanese restaurant where the real heavy hitters wined and dined. Anywhere from one to five hundred dollars was the going price for a dinner. The chefs were really Japanese, and cooked your food right in front of you, with true talent. The sauces, the knives, the spatulas…it was definitely a sight to see.

"You ever ate there?"

Tracey said, "This will be my first time."

"See, I'm ya guy," boasted Marlo. He couldn't disguise his arrogance or the confidence that seemed to ooze from him. Tracey would be the first woman he'd taken there in a while. "What time can I pick you up?"

They agreed on 8 PM Wednesday. She showed Marlo where she lived, which was right by the tennis courts. He walked her to the door which read F-12, checking her out in a way that she actually appreciated. His eyes were on her backside, her hair, Marlo even looked in Tracey's ears to see if she was really as clean as she looked.

"So Wednesday, I'll be ready, fly guy."

Marlo tried to kiss her on the cheek, and she back away saying, "Maybe Wednesday you can kiss me."

As soon as Marlo walked off, Tracey reached in her top for a phone. She hit call. As soon as she got an answer she said, "You aren't gon believe who I just met.

Marlo Reeves. And—he's a butt man. Couldn't keep his eyes off my derriere."

"There's a whole lot more to you than a marvelous *bootaaay*. Only if Marlo Reeves knew," the man returned laughing like the Joker in *Dark Knight*.

"We're going out Wednesday."

"Be careful. He may just want some butt."

Tracey didn't find that funny, and simply said, "Not all brother's think that way." Then she pressed END.

Chapter 11

Tuesday, and under the many skyscrapers down-town, about four blocks from Duke's east campus, Eva and Gloria sat outside in front of Devine's. It was a nice bar and grille on Main Street, where lawyers, Judges, City Hall employees, and even the Mayor enjoyed lunch from time to time.

Gloria was a 52-year old white woman with a 5'4" stature and weighed exactly 159 pounds. As far as her body, she was definitely stacked from head to toe, with one of those blonde hairdos that Jenifer Aniston wore. Gloria had an undeniable temptation for black men with a level of sophistication. Eva and Gloria were not only co-workers, they were almost sisters-in-law, because Gloria used to date one of Eva's brothers. Even though their relationship didn't work out, the two women remained close. By Gloria also being a certified public accountant, she did Eva a favor and handled the church's books for the Reverend.

As people strolled the city sidewalk and cars cruised by, Eva and Gloria sat at the gray marble style textured table and conversed under the shade from the sun.

"Eva, I was about to curse Trudy's ass out this morning," Gloria gossiped as she inhaled the fresh air.

"Gloria, what has Trudy done now? You two is always at each other's throats."

Trudy was also an accountant for the city. Since Gloria got promoted to Supervisor, Trudy always did what she could to piss off Gloria because she was always fraternizing with the coloreds. Gloria was fine with it, and could care less who did or didn't like it.

"Eva, I come into work this morning," Gloria began explaining, "and no one was at the coffee station. Then as soon as I head that way, she carries her *slender freckled face ass* over there and take her time making one cup of coffee. When has it ever taken someone ten minutes to make a cup of coffee??"

Before Eva could interject, Gloria went on saying, "I was about to blank on her. It was too early for that."

Eva said, "I know that's right." She then looked around for either a waiter or a waitress.

Once Gloria realized that Eva wasn't really interested in the Trudy drama, she dug into her hand into her expensive purse. "Here's your husband's money from Sunday's service. For some reason, the offering is declining." She knew that would get Eva's attention.

"Declining??? Gloria what does that mean?" Eva was rather shocked, and a couple of creases appeared

on her forehead as she observed the check Gloria had handed her.

"It seems as if the congregation is cutting back, when it comes to their tithing," Gloria shared, now too looking for a waiter. "Offering was no less than $25,000 a week." Having let that settle in, in a professional tone, she continued with, "That's how I've rounded it to the closest sum as far as amount. Once I pay the bills, take the money for the daycare, upcoming anniversaries, and my fee, your husband normally has seven thousand after Sundays' services. Now he's clearing only $5,800. Eva, if it's not the congregation, someone is stealing. I've been doing bookkeeping for twenty-seven years, and never have I seen a drop off of this fashion. You feel me, girl?"

"But, Gloria, Earl would've been said something to me," Eva replied as she continued to observe the digits on the check.

"Eva, he wouldn't know, because I've been giving him some of my fee to make it right. It's just since I've been putting Chad through college, I needed the money this week."

Eva watched Gloria sit back in the chair and run her fingers through her hair. She had no reason to doubt Gloria. "So what do I tell Earl?" Eva asked. "If I tell him, that's what Sunday's sermon will be about."

"Someone stealing, or the congregation cutting back?" Gloria asked.

Eva was concerned and saw the same all over her friend's face. Gloria said, "Let's give it another month, see if anything changes."

"Okay, Gloria," Eva said. "But please stay on it. What I'm going to do is go to my stash and make it right. The money will still be in the same household."

As Gloria agreed with Eva, they embraced. Then as they took their seats, a waiter arrived and took orders.

$ $ $

While Eva and Gloria got back to work, Marlo, Nu-Nu and Reverend Reeves sat in the dining room around the rectangular glass table for four, and conducted business as 97.5 played throughout the condo.

"Marlo, you know what time I get here. You suppose-ed have everything ready," the Reverend stated in a calm but very serious tone, with two large Louis Vuitton duffels sitting right before him. "You in here playing games and whatnot. Where is my money?"

"Unk, I got the loot," Marlo replied, as he listened to his uncle kindly ridicule his business savvy. "Any-way, we didn't expect you to be here until 1:30."

"Yeah, Unk," Nu-Nu lamented. "You crept up on us.

But the whole one-eighty is ready for you."

The Reverend was in a hasten mood because he hadn't exactly been feeling comfortable in the condo lately. And he also didn't like the way that woman in the yoga pants with the cute little dog was paying so much unwanted attention to him as he entered the complex. New faces gave him the chills lately. Even at Jubilee Baptist.

"How about getting it then. You know when I come over here, it's in and out," Reverend Reeves ordered, as he looked from Marlo to Nu-Nu. "Do you know my status in the community? Can't have you two slippin'."

Marlo looked at Nu-Nu as he got up from the table quickly, adhering to the order.

"Unk, what's wrong? We on point," Marlo deadpanned, as he watched Nu-Nu returning with identical duffels as the two sitting in front of the Reverend.

Reverend Reeves got real 'hood with Marlo—"Look, neph, I'm not trying to hear all that jazz." He then hit the table with a closed fist to match the fury in his words. "Be on point! That's all! Because, if I continue to feel that you're not moving right, I'm going to shut this shit all the way down. You dig?"

Marlo knew his uncle's words were bond. And he didn't want to lose out on his connections. It was basically easy free money in his eyes. Also, it was

Marlo's claim to fame in the streets. Just like Nu-Nu, he played it smart and kept his mouth shut. He let his uncle roar like a king would. And the Reverend was definitely king of that castle.

"You two laying up in here living large. At least you can respect my status. What do you have to lose?"

In his mind, Marlo was cursing the Reverend out. He knew that he and Nu-Nu could move on and do their own thing. It would be hard to influence Nu-Nu because the Reverend was Nu-Nu's mentor in more way than one. Earl didn't have any kids, so long before they began to play the game, he embraced his nephew like they were his own. While in prison, the Reverend wrote them encouraging them to not follow the path he had, warning them that there were bunks waiting for them if they did.

While Nu-Nu kept his mouth shut and remained humble, Marlo was fuming and still plotting. Visions of him over a stovetop with coke cooking in a vision ware pot invaded his thoughts. Then the quietness was broken when the doorbell rang. And—*raaaang*.

Panic was written all over the Reverend's face. He pushed the bags containing the $180,000 across the table first, then the ones with the blocks of coke. "Nu-Nu, hurry! Put these up. Marlo—you check that out."

Marlo moved the quickest he had ever in his life. He

He rushed for the love seat, flipped the cushion and retrieved a loaded pistol with a shiny nickel finish. The Reverend shut his eyes and said a silent prayer, as Marlo approached the door with the firearm tucked behind his right hamstring. With his right eye in the peephole, Marlo discovered that it was Tracey. Feeling relieved, he stalked back to the love seat, muttering, "What in the hell is she doing here on Tuesday???"

"What you say nephew?" the Reverend quizzed while watching Marlo push the weapon back up under the sofa cushion.

"I was talking to myself," Marlo replied.

"Marlo, who is it??? Damnit!!!" Reverend Reeves snapped with disdain for Marlo's facial expressions.

"It's a friend of mine," Marlo finally replied, as he strolled back to the door. "I wasn't expecting her. We're suppose to link up tomorrow night. She just moved here a couple weeks ago."

When the Reverend heard it was a woman, which happened to be one of his few weaknesses, he said, "Well, let her in. She's cool, right?"

Marlo was relieved that Reverend Reeves didn't flip out about strangers being on the premises. "Yeah, she cool, a banker out in Chapel Hill, Unk" he said.

Once Marlo unlocked the deadbolt and turned the door knob, and let Tracey in, the Reverend couldn't believe his eyes. Tracey wore a yellow Tee with OLD NAVY in big blue letters going across her bust, a pair of faded tight blue jeans, and Saucony running sneakers. Plain Jane for the day. "Tracey, what are you doing here?" Marlo asked through clenched teeth. "Our date isn't until tomorrow."

"I was off today and I was thinking, *I can't just walk by when I see your car out front.* Plus I can't get you out my mind," she whispered back with her breath smelling like a fresh piece of bubble gum.

Marlo could not contain the urge to grin. A sexy slim-thick babe thinking about him, and his uncle not being overbearing. This was the best day of his life.

Reverend Reeves looked at Marlo as if to say *Get the hell on!* Then he could grab his money and bounce.

As all those things were running through Marlo's mind, Tracey was casing the joint and taking mental notes. She made eye contact with the Reverend before telling Marlo, "I'm going to go. But once you are finish doing whatever it is that has your mind not on me, I'll be in front of my condo. Stop by."

And just like that, Tracey was gone.

As she left, the Reverend sweated Tracey's ass. He thought for a split second they were making a connection, as if she and Queenie weren't in the same tribe as far as physical features go. *The more you get, the more you want*, he silently reasoned.

Suddenly, his phone chirped. Looking at the caller ID, he saw that it was Queenie. She was right outside, waiting patiently in her car, so that they could get their evening started. Reverend Reeves always took Queenie to a Marriott Hotel in either Raleigh or Chapel Hill, which was out of Durham where they would go unnoticed. Especially since Queenie was a very affceti-onate woman, seeing nothing wrong with public displays of affection.

"Nu-Nu, bring the bags with the money," Marlo blurted out towards the loft where Nu-Nu had darted to when they heard the knocking. Marlo wanted to get his uncle up out of there so he could try to get with Tracey's fine ass.

Nu-Nu wasted no time, as he had something set up with Felita that he was trying to get to as well. With all the Reeves men thinking with their man meat, things kind of fell right back into place, as if they had never gotten on the Reverend's nerves.

After the Reverend closed the door, he headed down the steps and made his way to his 2017 money green Corvette with a black convertible top. As he strolled in his blue Ralph Lauren button down and beige khakis, he hit the alarm switch on his key and also pressed the trunk switch as well.

Queenie sat in her car and watched as he tossed the two duffels in the trunk, wondering what was in those heavy bags. And why in the hell that woman had come to visit her man. Oh, she couldn't wait to find out. Queenie was fuming.

"I'll be a mistress, but not a mistress to a mistress!

As the Reverend revved up the motor, he noticed Tracey sauntering up the sidewalk with a dog, and heading back towards the condo. It was then that he noticed that she was the same woman in the yoga pants who was watching him when he first pulled up. *Why had she changed clothes?* he wondered.

Watching the Reverend fasten his seatbelt and back out of his parking spot, Queenie fought back the urge to call him and begin her investigation right at that very moment.

But she decided to put it God's hands, and just slowly tailed the Corvette just as they had planned it.

Chapter 12

Out the Pioneer speakers, Foxy 107.1 played some relaxing R&B music, as Lawrence steered the wheel of his silver Mazda sedan. After a good workout with Lawrence, Rita sat on the passenger side and listened to Ronald Isley as he sang *"Between The Sheets"*. Riding shotgun down Trinity Ave, Rita was in a deep trance. She was still marveling about the trip to the gym.

As she rode in the sporty car beside Lawrence, Rita couldn't help but look over at her Romeo. .From his rough hands gripping the steering wheel, to his broad chest behind his seatbelt. What really amazed Rita was, out of all the physically fit women in Planet Fitness checking him out that day, not one time did Lawrence entertain them. His attention belonged to Rita, making sure she did her sets correctly and didn't quit. Lawrence had impressed Rita so much that she couldn't wait to hit the gym with him again.

Lord, put more men like Lawrence on the planet.

Even though he was driving, Lawrence could feel Rita's eyes all over him. As he maintained his focus on the road, Lawrence reached over and rubbed Rita's thick thigh, slowly easing his way to where her legs met on her blue Nike sweat shorts. Rita bit down on her bottom lip and embraced the idea of Lawrence craving her. He was planning on getting Rita a membership, so she could accompany him more often. Especially now knowing she got off at 2 PM in the evening.

"So, how are you feeling?" he asked Rita, breaking the silence and approaching a red light at the intersection of Trinity and Washington. "I know you're going to be sore tomorrow, after two hours of training."

"I'll be fine," Rita said tightening her thighs on Lawrence's hand.

He had Rita on the treadmill, doing jumping jacks, squats, curls, and light bench presses with 20 lbs dumbbells. He was just grooming her for the future, and removing any and all doubt that may've existed in her life. By the time they were done training, Lawrence knew Rita was 39, and all about her past relationship. That increased Lawrence's fondness of her, instead of making him judgmental. He now wanted to be part of Rita's life and all the struggles that may come with it. He saw Rita blow the roof off the church, so he knew she was ambitious and worth it. Being down himself once, he had a stronger notion to partner up with her.

The light turned green and Lawrence not only pulled off fast, but he pulled his hand from between Rita's legs as well. He could feel her grinding on his fingers and that was getting him aroused. He wanted to wait at least 90 days before he bedded Rita, or had any real intimate encounters with her. So there was no rush.

Suddenly huge raindrops began to crash into the windshield, as Lawrence continued to drive. Trinity Manor Apartments was still very visible up ahead.

"Rita, we are here," he chimed as he took a left into the parking lots of the big brick rundown apartment complex.

As soon as he pulled in, he noticed a young dark skinned guy with cornrows, about 15 years of age, run up to the car as if Lawrence was looking to cop. Lawrence was a bit offended, but at the same time, that was all the kid knew. Some women then came into Lawrence's view, all three aimlessly ambling and looking to turn a trick. Having once dealt drugs himself, and becoming his very own best tester and consumer, which was the cause of his lengthy prison term, Lawrence hated to see Rita holding residence there.

"Pull over out back," Rita instructed while directing Lawrence to a driveway leading to her building. "Keep looking to your left, and you'll see apartment 27. That's where I live."

Driving carefully, Lawrence noticed a scraggly white man pissing on the side of Rita's building. He saw three winos passing a wine bottle between them, as piss found its way beneath their rundown boots.

Rita was ashamed, and did a terrible job of hiding that shame from Lawrence. She had told him while they were working out that she lived all alone, but she didn't tell Lawrence how bad things were.

Rita once worked at the V.A. hospital. Due to her ex-boyfriend coming to her job on the regular and causing problems with the constant and loud profanities, the Human Resources Department told Rita that it was best that their employer and employee relationship cut ties. She lost a job that paid $19 an hour. Without any real savings in her bank account, unemployment was all she had. Then there was the daycare center that gave her a chance, for $10 bucks an hour, which beat nothing. *All because of a man who screwed another woman in her bed.* Trinity Manor kept Rita from being homeless.

Living in a halfway house, Lawrence understood her pain, and empathized with her. Pretty soon his time would be up, and post-release would put him in position to have his own place again. If Lawrence's moves coincided with his intentions for Rita, they could unite, wed, and build a nice home together. Overcoming the odds, Lawrence only knew one way—and that was up. It was kind of early for all those thoughts, so he snapped out of it.

"I guess I'll see you at choir rehearsal on Saturday," Lawrence said as he got set for Rita's departure, and ready to head on back to the halfway house before he missed curfew.

Rita just nodded with this warm smile on her face.

"How will you be getting there?"

"I am going to give you my number, so that you can

call anytime you want, and come by. I *meaaan,* come get me, for rehearsal."

Lawrence liked the sound of all that, and said, "I'll be here to get you Saturday, and I'll call you as soon as I get out the shower."

Rita had never been so courageous as to give a man her number, but there she was putting it into Lawrence's Galaxy phone. Even her ex-boyfriend didn't get her phone number. He had just popped up at her old apartment after a chance meeting at the local market. She let him in, and he had put that thing on Rita so good that he just never left, just moved in. No need for her number.

"Here you go," Rita said handing him back his phone, while secretly wishing Lawrence had just invited himself up like her old boyfriend had.

Lawrence smiled, leaned over, and caught Rita off guard with a kiss. He couldn't help himself, he had to tongue her down. Once their kiss came to an end, Lawrence and Rita both stared at one another, almost as if they were both awestruck.

"Oh, yeah," Lawrence remembered. "When I get to the spot, I'm going to call Earl and have a discussion with him about Keith."

Rita cheesed. "Please do, Lawrence. Because he gots to go. Honestly, we need Doug back."

"I got your back, Rita. Earl will listen to me. Understand, blood is thicker than water."

Then Lawrence stated as he opened the driver's side door, "Stay in the car. I don't' want you to get wet."

"But I'm already...*wetttt.*"

"*Huuhhhh?*"

"From when you touched my cookies."

Lawrence laughed as he retrieved an umbrella from the trunk of his car, thinking, *You still got it old fella!*

He opened the umbrella, walked around to the passenger door, and escorted Rita to her apartment with the umbrella over her head. Rita thought, *This is a fairy-tale.*

Not Lawrence getting her wet between the legs. Not him holding the umbrella over her head. Not her nosey neighbors seeing the romantic gesture that had her gushing. But Keith disappearing.

Chapter 13

Over on Dearborn Drive, and not too far from Braggtown projects was a smokehouse where local crack heads would congregate. And there was not an addict more important than Pokey at that address. Every fiend that came through there broke him off with a piece of their pleasures, as he was far more fortunate than they were. His product would have sparkling crystals glistening on it. And there he was, empty handed, high, and feeling deeply regretful.

He knew what he had done was wrong, as far as not taking full responsibility when it came to the possession of schedule II charge. Instead, he broke the code and sent the police Marlo's way. It was like he went into a phone booth being real, and came out an informant.

Ever since Pokey had that run-in with Officer Green, the police had been putting mad pressure on him, pumping him constantly for information on other operations out at the condos and elsewhere. Specifically other dealers, and even a cold homicide case. Green even brought Pokey a cell phone so he could keep tabs on him, and threatened him with jail time if he didn't answer. *I will throw you so far back in prison, that the state will have to transport sunlight to your ass!* The coldness in Green's voice shook Pokey to the core.

Pokey thought smoking coke nonstop would ease his worries. He knew what he'd done wouldn't just effect Marlo, but the entire Reeves clan. Guilt flowed all through Pokey's body. And the resident of the house, Mr. Sack, knew something was definitely bothering his buddy. "Look here, Pokey. When you gonna pull out the good stuff?" Sack asked sternly, while holding his pipe tightly. Pokey sat at the scratched brown kitchen table with a gram of *okay coke* broken up in little pieces.

"This ain't like you, Pokey."

Pokey continued to enjoy his daze, holding his crack pipe with both hands.

"I know you hear me talking to your ass, Pokey." Sack sat at the table across from him and continued to bass, "If you keep acting like you don't hear me, you can hit the road jack." Pokey smiled, as that was the least of Pokey's worries.

Sack was light skinned, 5'9", in his mid-fifties—just as the Reverend and Pokey were. The three of them grew up in East Durham together. When Sack enlisted into the Army, and came back, he kind of strayed off and was doing his own thing. They were still friends, but losing his wife and lifestyle caused Sack's to distant more than anything. He now lived off of Social Security, and whatever else having the most popping smokehouse may bring. Throughout the week, all day and night, people came to Sack's crib for their escape.

Ever since Pokey got busted, he's been laying low at Sack's crib. Pushing a $20 rock across the table to Sack, Pokey maintained a straight face. Sack continued to observe his buddy since Pokey normally conversed while beaming up. Sack also noticed Pokey didn't ask for the room with the big bed where all the kinky stuff went down. *Something is really on Pokey's mind*, Sack figured, *if he ain't trying to trick a skeezer.*

"Pokey, what in the hell is wrong with you?" asked Sack as he began to get high. "I'm ya boy. Talk to me."

Pokey sat quiet and paranoid. He couldn't discuss what was going on. Sack wouldn't hold water. Other than the cops, if anyone offered Sack some money or coke for information, he'd definitely drop it like it was hot. Especially if it benefited the peron's safety, because Sack hated snitches and slimeballs.

Changing the subject, Sack asked, "When is the last time you seen or heard from Earl? Still work for him?"

Pokey was coming down as he said, "Oh yea, still with ole Earl." He watched Sack take another toke, then added, "Just did something for him last week."

"Earl is doing it big," Sack replied as he smoke blew from his mouth and nose. "I was watching his ass on TV the other day. He had those people pumped up and giving him that paper. Earl needs to stop his mess. You know I know how he get down."

Pokey said nothing. The guilt was overwhelming.

There was a knock at the door, a soft one.

With a frenzied look, Sack got up. He walked over to the kitchen counter and put his pipe in the kitchen drawer. "Put that shit up," he mouthed to Pokey.

Sack quickly moved across the dirty tiles, in a wife-beater, cutoff shorts, and some ankle socks. Approaching the door, he pulled the blue towel back. A quick ganger revealed that it was Laverne. *She must've turned a trick or two, and came to turn me on,* Sack thought.

"Hey boo," Laverne blurted, making her way across the threshold in a brand new Gloria Vanderbilt blouse and tight jeans. Even though Sack's floor hadn't been cleaned in days, Laverne still kicked her gray stilettos off her feet. "You know it's me! The Diva. I told you I was coming back." She then turned and saw Pokey at the table. "Oh, word is out about you, *mister*," she shot at Pokey as she tiptoed to the table. She pulled up a chair and sat right across from him.

"Yvonne is pouring salt on your ass," she sounded off while checking Sack out. Laverne was in good shape to be a smoker. She had long black naturally curly hair to go with her smooth cinnamon complexion. Laverne was six feet tall and could've modeled professionally had she not been introduced to free-base back in the 90's. The young trappers often tried to trick her. But she had a son in his teens, and would never want that to be a narrative that could affect him. *Yo momma out there tricking young boyz!* Instead, she used her vibrant looks to trick tricks who didn't want it out there. Like

Councilmen, attorneys, and other public officials.

"Pokey, I knew it was something!" Sack immediately shouted. "What in the hell did you do to Yvonne??? I don't want no shit up in my crib!"

Pokey just looked on.

"That girl got some crazy brothers! And from what I hear, they're Bloods!"

Pokey still said nothing.

"Pokey!" both Sack and Laverne shouted.

"I ain't did shit to Yvonne," Pokey finally replied in a puzzling tone. "Laverne, what in the hell is you talking about? Stirring shit up?"

Sack looked to Laverne, and she said, "I ain't stirring up nothing. I love my face, and I don't need no one trying to fuck it up. Yvonne put the word out that you two were in your van getting high in the projects and the cops ran up on you two. The word on the streets is, you got busted with damn near an eight-ball and didn't go to jail at all, not even for one day. So is that true?"

"Yeah, is it true?" Sack asked with his arms folded across his chest, and then back at Laverne as if he were the judge and making credibility assessments. He knew Laverne was a streetwalker and her word was golden when it came to situations with the police.

"So, I'm not saying you did or didn't. But Yvonne is making you look like a rat," Laverne made clear, as she dug her hand into her bra and pulled out some rock. "All I'm saying is, stay out the projects, Pokey."

Sack continued to eye Pokey and Laverne. He wasn't sure what to do. *Believe her, or remove Pokey from the kingdom???*

Pokey felt it, and could only sigh.

Chapter 14

3 YEARS

EARLIER ...

It was a Sunday, and an icy one. The year was 2015, one of the rare times Durham experienced snowfall of that magnitude. So the Reverend decided to drive his Range Rover and used the 4-wheel drive feature to maneuver the slush and ice. Eva was riding shotgun, like she always had, and in her Sunday's best. The Reverend was sharp too.

When they arrived at Jubilee Baptist Church, the Reverend perked up a bit. The place was packed. Surely it was a site to see. The Reverend was living his dream, and Eva loved it. A determined man, moving with purpose and preaching the word. And—the Reverend was easy on the eyes. Eva didn't need to notice the extra attention the Reverend's presence generated amongst the many women of the congregation, to know Earl was the sexiest man in Durham. Since her high school years, Eva could identify a good looking man when she seen one.

"*Earl*," Eva called in a pleasant tone.

"Yes, darling," the Reverend responded, pulling slowly and carefully up to his reserved spot.

"That truck looks just like yours," Eva replied, pointing her fancy fingernail to the right of their vehicle.

The Reverend peeked at the rearview mirror, and sure enough, a triple black 2014 *4.6* model was parked on the church's property. The Reverend wondered who had upgraded, but more importantly, why hadn't that person chosen a different color. He had a sermon to deliver, and nothing was more important than that. But, the Reverend vowed to complement the owner for having good taste, because that was the right thing to do. *Magnify his image, in the name of God, and not appear petulant.*

...Things had gone well that blessed Sunday. The newest singer, Rita possessed a big voice to match her size and personality. The Reverend had met Rita during a counseling session, and learned that her true passion wasn't bad boys, it was singing. That was the day Reverend Reeves decided the choir would be backing up Rita.

Having concluded his praised of Rita, he asked her, "Who's driving the Range Rover?"

"I don't know, Reverend," Rita stated, then promised, "I'll ask around."

"That would be me, Reverend," a smooth voice interjected from just a few feet away. "I was feeling the message in the sermon you delivered today."

"And who might you be?"

Before the fellow could properly introduce himself to the Reverend, the Reverend said, "Here at Jubilee Baptist, I know all of my members on a first and last name basis. And I've never encountered you here, or in Durham."

The fellow wasn't wearing his Sunday's best. Instead, he was dressed as if he was the fourth member of the rap group *Migos*. But his accent was lacking the ever familiar southern drawl. So the Reverend knew that this guest was an out-of-towner, which further heightened his curiosity.

"Edward Haywood, of the Bronx, New York," the fellow conveyed, extending his hand for the Reverend's.

While shaking Edward's hand, and with Rita spectating, the Reverend said, "And what brings you to Jubilee Baptist, Edward Haywood from the Bronx?"

"Well, change brought me to Durham, and to Jubilee Baptist," replied Edward, as he turned his attention to Rita. "And, ... if she's gonna be singing here."

"What changes are you looking to make, Edward?"

"One second, Reverend Reeves," Edward began, then turned to Rita. "Miss Rita, have you ever thought about cutting a record?"

Rita noticed Edward's Rolex, and that the Reverend had the same bezel. She also noticed the Reverend's eyes sending her off.

When Rita vanished through the corridor, Edward said, “Just a different lifestyle. A fresh start, Rev.”

Reverend Reeves learned that Edward was pushing thirty, married with two children, two drug convictions for which Edward had served three years as a juvenile, and a plethora of charisma to go with the Range and the watch. Edward didn’t lie when the Reverend asked about the lavish amenities. He said, “I’m a plug…who wants out, sir.”

Edward became a standing member of Jubilee Baptist Church, a legitimate businessman in the community, and the jumper cable that brought the old Earl back to life…

BACK TO THE *PRESENT…*

Marjorie was splayed across her California king bed watching *The Young and The Restless*. Her favorite soap opera. The blue comforter with Gucci symbols all over it felt good, but the Reverend’s presence would have felt better. Knowing Eva worked weekday, Marjorie took her eyes from the 48” Phillips plasma screen television mounted to the wall and grabbed her smart phone. Her screen saver was still a photo of her and the Reverend she got off his Facebook page. The photo was cropped now. Instead of Eva holding his chiseled bicep, Marjorie was on his arm. Eva's sexy body, *but Marjorie's still elegant face.*

Marjorie was helpless in her thoughts of the Reverend going ballistic when she returned from her walk-in closet in just the shoes she'd purchased that day at the mall. To this day, Marjorie doesn't know what made her do it. But she was glad she had, because the Reverend couldn't resist the temptation, and mercilessly mounted Marjorie as she hoped he would. The Reverend didn't just know what he was doing, he did it well.

With that in mind, she sought pleasure by texting the Reverend –

Thank u for u know what…

And then instead of waiting for the reply, Marjorie slipped her right hand up under her Victoria Beckham evening gown and pleasured herself.

Who says a woman in her fifties can't still be erotic??? Marjorie was just hitting her sexual peak.

The Reverend didn't text back, and Marjorie began trying to figure out how to get ahold of the Reverend.

The urge of something more with the Reverend was taking hold of her, and loneliness was no longer a figment of her imagination, but a harsh reality she had a hand in creating. Even though her late husband had been unfaithful, he never ignored her calls. However, Marjorie was a widow of wealth and grace, so no one else would do. She wanted Reverend Reeves. *Period!*

The way she was cropping photos and gazing at them, if the Reverend could see this, he would certainly question his wife's safety, as well as his own. *And* he could handle himself pretty well. He just didn't know that Jimmy Dean he put on Marjorie was a really bad decision. *The Young and The Restless* had gone off and there still was no reply from him. But Marjorie wasn't about to tap out because of unanswered calls and texts. Marjorie was a wily veteran in the patience department, as well as creating diversions.

The marriage vows the Reverend and Eva shared may've meant something to them and the congregation, but they meant nothing to Marjorie.

The doorbell rang, startling her. Marjorie wasn't expecting anyone. No deliveries, no maintenance work, no friends, so she was tempted to continue pleasuring herself with the Reverend's image just inches from her eyes. But, the doorbell rang again. She cleaned up quickly, then descended to the ground level by way of the spiral staircase. She approached the double doors to her lovely but lonely abode, still wondering who would show up unexpected.

Marjorie couldn't believe her eyes.

Chapter 16

Monday through Saturday, from 8 in the morning to 9 at night, *Sparkle's Hair Salon* doors were open to the public. From weave and braids, to the hottest crop cuts, manicures and pedi's, *Sparkles's* was the spot. The stylists were always on their A-game, and women of all races and ethnicities preferred the downtown spot on Riggsbee over any other salon in town. With the spas, and music videos on the many mounted monitors, and the constant gossip mill that never seemed to end, what woman wouldn't want to be made fabulous there???

The scent of expensive perfumes, hair products, polishes and nail removers permeated the air, while the sounds of driers and laughter and chatter blended with the sounds of grown folk music.

Keith's chair was never empty. His clientele would sit in their cars or post up outside if Sparkle's had yet to open its doors. He always had a days work cut out for him, so appointments were necessary unless you were Queenie, or the R&B Diva Fantasia. On this particular day his appointment had his fingers cramping. "Kathy, I've done tried to catch this short shit and hook a braid to it"—he was attempting to freak some micro braids—"but it ain't working," he blurted to the pintsize mocha brown sistah in his chair. "You need to go with the *Toni Braxton do*, girllll."

Keith's voice traveled so instantly laughter erupted. He pulled in anywhere from $400 to $600 daily, so he didn't give two cents about putting a chick on blast. His appointment list was booked for the next two weeks too.

"No, Keith! I already had micros in my hair before," Kathy chided with no intentions to changing course. Keith stood right over top of her with a wicked snarl on his grill. "Remember, Keith??? You put them in???"

"I know, Kathy," Keith shot back loving the attention. "However, your shit is not catching today. Your braids are breaking off. I mean, damn—can't do it."

"Just forget it, Keith—"

"Forgotten!" Keith shot back removing the cape from her neck and perky chest.

"I'll go to Bev's Salon over in Lakewood Shopping Center! She can do it."

"She's mad at me because I can't do the impossible," Keith snapped. The truth was, he was unable to focus. He didn't like the way Queenie had dismissed him when he mentioned his hostile takeover of the choir. She had never gone against him in the past. And that was weighing heavy of his mind. As the girl was storming out the salon with her cute yellow sundress, Keith followed her. He apologized for being rude, then offered her a do on him next week.

"Fine," Kathy said just as another woman walked up.

"Kissie, it's good to see you, and my chair is empty," Keith said while Kathy jumped in her convertible Benz.

"Good, because I have a lot on my mind."

As Keith walked her inside, he asked, "About what? What is it? Men again???"

"This singing at the church thing. I don't know that I'm equipped for it. I have been asking around, and there seems to be a lot of people who like the Rita girl."

As Kissie sat in his chair, Keith watched with his hands stuffed into the pockets of his designer skinny jeans. He began to wonder was he doing the Lord's work in trying to replace Rita, or was this just his own selfish ways reemerging because he was feeling bored and incomplete?

To change the topic and to give himself sometime for a comeback, he slipped a fresh cape over Kissie, and said, "Damn, your shit is tangled up. You just left here last week. Why's your hair so kinky?"

"Kiss my ass, Keith," Kissie shot back brandishing her feisty side. They both laughed, then he said, "I feel you, as those are some big shoes to fill, and I mean literally. But if anyone can do it, you can. And there is this fine brother named Edward Haywood that I think you might like. He's from New York, and he's solid."

Kissie perked up. She knew who Edward was. And bets believe Keith noticed it. "He owns his own businesses and all that, girlfriend," Keith added.

"He sounds very interesting," she boohooed.

Keith had never really spoken to Edward, yet he knew a lot about him. He knew a whole lot more than people thought he did. But he would never step out of line. Keith even felt this sudden guilt for using Edward to bait Kissie. But it was game on.

Kissie on the other hand, wasn't really looking for a come up like most women did when they find out a brother is about his business. She was 27-years-old, and tired of guys promising her record deals if she would sleep with them. Kissie had been singing for a little over a decade, had even performed for J. Cole once. However, Edward Haywood and Kissie under the same church roof just may lead to something special.

"I'll be there Saturday," Kissie said as Keith began to give her the treatment he'd become famous for.

"Please do, because the way you *sang*, Reverend Reeves might just be knocked off his feet! You sound just like Yolanda Adams! It's gonna be a surprise to him, the choir and the congregation."

$ $ $

Outside on Marjorie's porch was a white man accompanied by a very shapely African American woman. They had emerged from a large black sedan, and appeared to be there on some serious business.

"Marjorie Wall, I'm Officer Green, and this is my partner. So, some new information concerning your late husband has become available to the authorities. And we would like to just ask you a few questions."

"Oooh," Marjorie replied as she opened the doors a bit wider. "Come right on in..."

$ $ $

Meanwhile, Reverend Reeves was in his Navigator pulling up to his designated parking space, with the steering wheel in one hand and his phone in the other.

"Listen, Lawrence...Keith isn't going anywhere, and neither is Rita," he stated for the third time with his phone just inches from his mouth. "I don't' know what you, Rita and Keith got going on, but I'm sure we can figure it out without unnecessary conflicts." Before Lawrence could say anything else, the Reverend ended the call. He was already pissed about the text Marjorie had sent to his phone. *What if Eva had seen this???* And now Lawrence was calling him suggesting things.

In frustration, he exited his truck and slammed the door shut before realizing too much emotion was being shown. Almost in an instant, he was back to being reserved, and seemingly in control. Heading towards four big brass doors, he deleted Marjorie's racy text message, then he stuck his key in and unlocked the main door. Entering the church, he quickly punched in the pass-code on the keypad to disable to alarm.

There was no singing and shouting, no preaching and

praising, only quietness. During the week, Reverend Reeves would go to the altar alone, just himself and God Almighty, get on his knees and repent his sins. None too small, nothing too big. Afterwards, he would look around at the sanctuary that God had bestowed upon him, and lift his hands in thanks, with the LUKE, CHAPTER 18, VERSE 25 in mind: *"Indeed, it is easier for a camel to go through the eye of a needle than for someone who is rich to enter the Kingdom of God."*

Reverend Reeves could hear God talking to him. With the motto in mind that, *Nobody is or ever will be perfect as the Lord.* That had become his reservation of excuse. He would then proceed to his office, look over the books and upcoming events on the calendar. Once all that was solidified, he would began preparations for Sunday's sermon.

He happened to be at his desk when another text registered from Marjorie:

Earl, I need you…

"This has to stop!" he shouted. The last thing he wanted was to be in the shower and have Marjorie's suddenly brazen behavior destroy his marriage. Deleting them wasn't going to stop Marjorie, only replying would, so he called her back and asked her to come to the church so that they could talk in person. He could see that laying hands on her had turned out to be a very big mistake.

$ $ $

Not even an hour later, Marjorie showed up in a hot red Altuzzara top and skirt she had spent a grip on. The black T-strap sandals she chose to wear were expensive too, and showed off a perfect pedicure. *She had been paying very close attention to her exterior lately, and very little attention to her interior*, thought the Reverend as he watched her saunter into his presence. He also forgot about cancelling her out, and led her to his office before even saying a word.

As Marjorie followed watching his hindquarters and broad back rather closely, she also held back her words.

The Reverend had been unable to control himself upon entering his office, which looked like a luxurious suite. Marjorie noticed the erection trying to break from his slacks when he turned to face her.

"Have a seat," he suggested with his right hand extended towards a black leather loveseat. Marjorie chose the long sofa instead. The Reverend continued to stand in a plaid Duck Head button up short sleeve shirt, and beige khakis. He stood in deep lust as he watched Marjorie cross one leg over the other showing her smooth legs. "So, what's going on?"

"Reverend Reeves," Marjorie began in a slow succulent tone. "Have a seat." She patted the loveseat.

The Reverend did, and she went on saying, "I've been trying to get hold of you all day, and I usually don't do that, impose my will, you know. Why haven't you replied? Why haven't I heard from you since our, you know, introduction to our lesser selves?"

"I've been doing the Lord's work," he fibbed, leaning into her intoxicating aroma. "And nothing or no one can interfere with that."

"Oh," Marjorie returned as she had fallen for that one. Her late husband had used that one before. "You do have big responsibilities."

"Yes! Exactly!" The Reverend was even more excited now, thinking he'd gotten a fast one over on her.

"Well, I've been missing you, and I wanted to apologize for seducing you." She was talking about when she had emerged from her walk-in closet in just some shoes. All in all, had the Reverend not been in her bedroom, she wouldn't have had the gall to try him.

"No need. And from now on, call me Earl like you did in the text—*but no more text*—when it's just me and you. Cool?"

Marjorie's left brow furrowed, *No more text???*

Once again he was abusing his power when leaned over and slipped his tongue in Marjorie's mouth while his left hand found its way up under her skirt. Feeling Marjorie's curly landing strip beneath her bikini cut panties, his erection felt as if it was going to bust the zipper open. He fingered her, kissed her, pressed up on her. And she was moved in a way she hadn't expected to have been. She was ambushed by passion and ecstasy, and her legs swung open welcoming him as her head fell back and away from his hungry mouth. Before she knew what hit her, the Reverend's mouth was buried between her thick thighs lapping at her slick opening making her squirm and moan. She felt tears of joy fall from her orbs and sighed with his head in her hands directing traffic. *There is goes!* she mused as her first orgasm met his face with a rush.

Unzipping his pants, he couldn't hold back. He wanted to experience that same sensation, and freed his magic stick. Hurriedly, he positioned Marjorie to his liking, her legs on his shoulders, and slowly slipped inside. Marjorie's eyes rolled to back of her head as Reverend Reeves began smashing her with every inch and from every angle. "Oh baby, where have you been?? Never hold this loving back from me this long again, *Earl*. Yes, *Earl*! I love this. And I love you."

With every word Marjorie moaned, Earl, *not the Reverend*, crushed her sweet gash. With the feeling of her sweet juices flowing all over his penis, he released her breasts so he could suck on them. *Implants aren't so bad!* he thought while tonguing her nipples feverishly. Her next orgasm flowed, and after her tremors and trembling, they bucked back at each other so he could get his. *And that he did.* Marjorie could feel him pulsating insider her, his jizm coating her insides, and felt a connection that was unimaginable.

Then they looked at each other. On the wall behind the Reverend's desk, and over his many certificates and degrees, hung Jesus on the cross realizing he wasn't the only one to be crucified. Easing her legs from his shoulders, he tucked his manhood back into his zipper. The front of his pants were soaked with Marjorie's releases.

"You did say I can call you Earl, right?" Marjorie asked after redoing her makeup.

The Reverend was readjusting his tie, a fancy one Queenie had picked up for him while they were rendezvousing in Chapel Hill, NC, the other day. "I did say that, Marjorie," he told her in a low pitch.

Marjorie was hesitant at first, because she didn't want to hurt the Reverend's feelings. But when she was done smoothing out her skirt, abruptly, Marjorie said, "Earl, I didn't come here for that."

"I know—I called you over."

"Right before you called, the authorities were out at my house," Marjorie explained.

The Reverend was looking down at the mess all over the front of his pants when Marjorie revealed that. He looked up and said, "Ahh—for what?"

"My late husband," she whimpered. "I've been informed that it's no longer a cold case."

The Reverend said, "Well, that's good news. Isn't it? Don't you want his killer brought to justice?"

The Reverend had done Marjorie's husband's eulogy, and thought the guy did really well in the business world for a man who wasn't the best husband.

"Would you miss me, if I left town?" Marjorie questioned while shuffling through her oversized Louis Vuitton bag.

As she was cleaning herself with a wet-wipe, the Reverend said, "Why would you leave town?"

There was a pregnant pause, a spider could be heard spinning a web in the attic, and then Marjorie resumed sanitizing her flesh.

They were both in this secluded proximity of space, bewildered by what had been pronounced from both sides. It was clear, the Reverend would not miss Marjorie, and had a stronger possibility of re-honoring his vows if she was gone. Marjorie, on the other hand, hoped she would have gotten a better and more caring response.

There was also this part of Reverend Reeves that desired to know *why* Marjorie was contemplating the sudden departure.

Marjorie had been in the church for so long, even before the Reverend's arrival. When others questioned his affirmation, she had been his staunchest supporter, preaching the need for new and savvier leadership.

While the Reverend pondered, Marjorie realized she still hadn't answered the million dollar question.

"Earl."

"Yes, Marjorie."

"Can I trust you? Not just as a lover, or friend, but as

my spiritual advisor?"

"Sure, sure, Marjorie," the Reverend quickly affirmed. The look on Marjorie's face told him this was about to get juicy.

"My life may be in danger—and it's all because of that winch posting them half-naked pictures on Instagram!" Marjorie stammered.

"Wait, wait—I'm lost, Marjorie."

Marjorie pulled out her phone, found the I.G. icon, and before they knew it, the Reverend was looking at racy photos of an insanely attractive woman with 190,000 followers. Nearly as much as the entire Durham population.

"Did she kill, Lewis?" the Reverend asked.

Marjorie burst into tears, spilling them all over the Reverend's collar and fresh tie. She looked up at the Reverend and told him, "If she disappears, I won't have to leave town. I can stay here with you, and we can continue building our life together."

"I'm really confused now, Marjorie," he returned as he took a step back.

"Nu-Nu and Marlo; they could take care of it, and make her disappear," Marjorie suggested.

"Excuse me, Marjorie?" the Reverend quipped, though it wasn't a laughing matter.

You didn't think I endorsed you because of your looks, did you? Supported you all these years because I didn't think there were more qualified men, did you?

Or, that this affair we are having was by chance?" Marjorie spoke rather eloquently.

Before the Reverend could say anything, she went on saying, "I know all about the activity out at Strawberry Hills. Those nephews of your sure ain't *house sitting*."

"My nephews are good boys!" the Reverend defended. "And I would never employ them to make anyone *disappear*. You're talking like those mafia guys back east." He paced, shaking his head. "If this woman killed Lewis, let the authorities do their job. Street justice has no place in my life, nor should it in yours, Marjorie."

Marjorie's well thought out plan hadn't worked the way she'd envisioned. She'd given Reverend Reeve's far more credit than he actually deserved. In fact, the Reverend wasn't ruthless at all, just a bit reckless. The Reverend was also more cerebral than she had ever imagined. So it didn't take him long to figure out exactly what Marjorie wasn't saying.

"Marjorie, I think you had better leave town," Reverend Reeves reluctantly advised. "Maybe the country, before the wall close in on you."

Marjorie immediately fixed her top and stormed off. She had never been spoken to that way. *Who did he think he was???* Not even a minute after she left, a seductive image of Queenie popped on his iPhone.

What does she want?

After displaying an even-keeled demeanor with a very dangerous woman, all the Reverend wanted to do was shower, and then go home.

$ $ $

Meanwhile, Marlo and Tracey sat in the living room of her condo on a gray plaid sofa that Marlo did not like. He didn't like her brass glass coffee table either. Or the brass throw lamp. And he could not hide his disdain. If she was going to be his lady, changes would have to be made. *Not even a TV?* First she was trying to explain why she hadn't answered her phone earlier when Marlo was calling. Then she was being interrogated about the lack of decorum in her condo. Tracey was ready to throw him out, but she knew she couldn't. So instead she answered with, "I'm waiting for my next paycheck, then I'm going to really jazz the place up."

Marlo walked away pulling his jeans up on his narrow ass. He then pulled his phone from his back pocket. Tracey looked on dumbfounded. He bent a corner and was in the kitchen area. Tracey got up and tiptoed over to try and listen to his conversation. *Maybe it's something noteworthy about to be said.*

"Yeah, man, I need a TV, with a glass cabinet and a DVD player. ASAP!"

He had called one of his boys who held employment at Best Buy. His boy said, "I got a 64 inch Samsung wit the plasma screen. I got you, *boss man*. When do you need this?"

"I said ASAP."

"Give me the address. I can get it done now for a little something extra. Not for me, but for the delivery guy."

"Cool." Marlo gave him the address, his credit card info, then ended the call.

Tracey dipped back to her seat, threw one leg over the other, then gave Marlo the best side of her face. No one had ever done anything like that for her. Nothing even close. She was startled.

They spoke a bit more, and Tracy tried to play it off like she was surprised when the doorbell rang. Like the man, Marlo sat and watched that loose ass bounce and shake with each step she took. He couldn't wait to get a piece of that.

Tracey opened the door without even asking who it was. "Delivery for, Marlo," the delivery guys said in unison.

Tracey saw them unloading and looked back, saying, "Marlo, you didn't have to do this."

He rose up. "That's how I get down. Believe this, I claimed you as my Queen when I laid eyes on you." As she blushed, he added, "That fat ass too."

Marlo always spoke his mind. After spending $347 on dinner the other night, dropping nearly a grand at

Best Buy, and not having even seen Tracey naked yet, Marlo felt he had the right to express himself in style.

"Boy, you is off the chain," Tracey chimed, cozying up to Marlo as they watched the delivery guys set everything up. "So now you're gonna come out your mouth like that?" She couldn't help but laugh.

"Shit, why not?" Marlo replied, chuckling at the same time. "I can't help it that you got a fat ass. Thank the Lord, and shake what your momma gave ya."

Tracey burst out into a hearty laughter. "Marlo," she cooed, as she hit him on his arm with a flirtatious tap.

Tracey was a country girl from a small town in North Carolina, with a population of 4,000. She wasn't use to men flashing and flexing their quick cash. In fact, she had been kept away from all that.

"All I'm doing is giving credit where credit is due. Check this out, … I know we've just met and all that, but I feel something special in my heart for you."

The truth was, Marlo saw something in Tracey he hadn't seen in a woman since he was a young-buck. That was—truth and honesty.

Of course, her physical features marveled him, but she appeared to be whole, not fragile and broken. And most of all, certain of herself, not lost.

"You see, you're so used to niggas spitting game from all I've gathered from our conversations. But, like I told you, I'm different from the rest. I'm the best."

Marlo was even caught off guard by what he had said.

He was letting it flow but for some reason, this was a much different flow than usual. Deep down inside, he knew that it was the exotic weed he'd smoked before he hooked up with Tracey. No matter what, he was going to let it flow.

Tracey was all in now. She didn't move away from Marlo, or get up off the sofa. Just that fast, Tracey was caught up and feeling Marlo. Thinking about his hospitality, the gifts and the dinner, Tracey was experiencing feelings and emotions she didn't know existed. In fact, Tracey began to feel guilty about what she was hiding from Marlo. The thought of how he would feel if it ever came down to it...if she decided to choose a side...and it not be his side...how devastated he would be. Life wasn't fair, ...but tomorrow would come...and today was all that mattered at that moment.

Tracey was in a daze when Marlo blurted, "Tracey, are you still with me??? Earth to Tracey!!!"

"Yes, of course," Tracey stammered.

"Dammn, you was gone," Marlo cackled. "What was you thinking about?"

"Just in deep thought. That's all." She rose from the sofa saying, "Give me a couple minutes. I've gotta use the bathroom."

Watching Tracey get up, Marlo said, "Good God Almighty." Before she could evade his range, Marlo slapped her on her backside, and laughed as it jiggled.

Tracey quickly armed herself with one of the pillows,

hit Marlo upside his head, and took off through the condo, heading towards the bathroom, giggling all the way. She felt like a high school girl liking a boy for the very first time. Leaning over the arm of the sofa, Marlo enjoyed a clear view of her ass as it bounced in the black yoga pants she was wearing.

Once she opened the door to the bathroom, her dog raced out and headed straight to Marlo's sent. As Tracey shut the door, she could hear Marlo playing with the canine. She stood just a foot from the mirror on the back of the door, took in the image staring back at her, thinking, *why am I falling for this guy???*

Chapter 17

FRIDAY MORNING...

Pokey was laid out across Sack's tattered brown leather sofa with his cell ringing nonstop. It was a miracle he had survived Laverne's character assassination attempt. That day they had got so high, Sack wound up in the big bed with Laverne. With Officer Green now blowing up Pokey's phone, he wasn't sure what may transpire. Sack's eyes were all over him, so he decided to send all calls straight to voice mail.

"Pokey, why ain't you answer that phone?" Sack asked while seated in the matching recliner while watching *Gunsmoke*. "I'm starting to think you're hiding out over here or something, Pokey," Sack added when Pokey failed to respond. "Laverne might be telling the truth about your ass, because you ain't never around this long."

Normally when people ran out of dope they would either leave, or Sack would put them out. Even though Pokey and Sack grew up together, Sack had no sympathy when the dope was gone. Pokey was his homey and all that, but it was time for him to go.

Sack asked, as he held his remote, "I thought you told me that you worked for Earl???"

"I do work for Earl," Pokey shot back as he continued to lay across the couch, right ankle over the left, and with his palms up under his head.

"Shit! I can't tell," Sack replied, throwing a hint so Pokey would leave. "Don't you think that you need to go home, wash, and change clothes. You can't go to work in that condition. I smell you way over here. You smell like *Old English*."

As if Pokey could afford anymore misfortune; his phone rang again.

"Pokey, answer that shit!" Sack commanded. "Might be Earl, seeing why you ain't at work!"

Pokey got tired of hearing Sack's mouth and sat up on the couch. Taking his hat off and rubbing his head, Pokey was contemplating his next move.

"Ain't no need in thinking, Pokey. You know that I'm telling the truth. You need to get yourself together."

How can this negro talk about me? All he do is sit around all day waiting for somebody to come in and turn him on! thought Pokey, fuming. *Sack ain't hitting on shit. Sitting around on his ass waiting for a check once a month. If it wasn't for his wife passing, he wouldn't have a damn thing.*

"Hey! Hey!" Sack sneered, interrupting Pokey's ill thoughts. "You know that's Earl calling you. Gone and answer the phone, man. You can't help me, if you don't help ya'self."

Pokey had had enough, and blurted out, "How in the

hell you know that's Earl calling me?" He then got up. "Other people call me."

"Well, it can't be nobody but Marlo, then," Sack retorted. He was pissed. "Shit! I'm tired of hearing that phone of yours ring back to back. I can't even enjoy my show."

"Sack, you just want me out. It ain't got nothing to do with this damn phone." Pokey tossed it at the wall, and it didn't break for some reason. "That's how you are. Dope gone, company gots to go too. I know your game."

Sack watched as Pokey retrieved the phone from the floor and examined it. "You can't get the hell out. Four days of laying up in here is enough. Or, you can sell the phone, so we can get high? It's up to you!"

Pokey just shook his head.

"People can't even enjoy their high, because of you. See, Laverne ain't been back."

"She ain't been back because you want her to get you high, then you want some sex for free. She's a working girl important people pay good money to be with."

Sack leaped from the recliner and tossed the remote on the faded brown coffee table. "What's up, then???" Sack was furious. "I'll bring smoke up out yo funky ass. You better be gone when I get back." Sack stormed off to his bedroom.

Watching Sack make his move, Pokey walked to the kitchen, quickly opened the back door, and darted to his van. Once he opened the door, got in, and keyed the ignition, Pokey put his van in reverse and backed out of Sack's driveway.

Seeing Sack came out the door with a Remington 12 gauge pump shotgun. No matter if cars were coming or not, Pokey tore ass up Dearborn Drive.

"You better left, *nut*!" Sack yelled, brandishing his weapon of choice in the air at the same time. "I was gonna put some pellets in that ass."

Pokey's van was halfway down the block and Sack was still fuming. As Pokey's van floated above the speed limit, he wondered where to go to get his thoughts in order. He considered just coming clean, and requesting that the Reeves boys get him out of town. But then the consequences registered that he had already gave up some names. He could be floating in the river out of town for his sins. Besides the Reeves, Pokey had only his elderly mother. He had burned so many bridges down, he wasn't surprised he was alone in those streets.

To no surprise, the phone was buzzing again. The screen read UNKNOW. Officer Green wasn't going away. *Maybe I should sell the phone.*

$ $ $

LATER THAT EVENING...

Over in the classy Pepper Tree Community, Reverend Reeves and Queenie lazed across her queen sized *Tomorrow* comfort bed. The soft brown ruffled country styled comforter covered half their bodies while Luther Vandross crooned one of his many classics. *If Only One Night.* They loved their oldies.

Queenie asked rather curious, and as she snuggled beside the Reverend in a red silk Christian Dior teddy with her hand propped under her head, "Babe, what made you just pop up over here today?"

Reverend Reeves said, "*This did,*" then leaned his head up and tongued Queenie's pretty mouth. She kissed him back.

But Queenie knew better. The Reverend would never just pop up without first calling. Whenever he did, it was something bothering him that he preferred sharing with Queenie instead of the first lady. They had a connection on certain issues of life that Eva would never understand.

Queenie pulled back from the Reverend's passionate smooch and inquired more. In a *stop bullshitting me* tone, she said, "Something is bothering you, and you're going to tell me, Earl."

Reverend Reeves had on a gray shirt that was unbuttoned, revealing a crisp T-shirt, and a pair of black Calvin Klein slacks that was unfastened. He was comfortable and experiencing peace when Queenie added to her words by straddling him. The comforter fell from them exposing Queenie's plump hindquarters, and the Reverend's hands didn't hesitate to cup them.

"What is on your mind, old man? Tell me...*now*."

"Nothing, babe," the Reverend shot back, while taking in Queenie's beauty.

Queenie began to grind in slow sensuous motion. She took the Reverend's hands off her behind, and place them on her full breasts. She loved the way he caressed them so passionately. Nowadays, men weren't as passionate or attentive. "I can feel when something's on your mind. Now tell me, or you're not getting any." Again, she rotated her pelvis all up against his manhood while looking him directly in the eyes.

Knowing Queenie wasn't going to stop seducing him, or pumping him for information, until he talked, he said, "I got a call from Lawrence the other day, and one from Rita today. Your brother's causing problems in the choir. And I can't have that, babe."

"Earl. I told you from the get-go, not to let Keith direct the choir," Queenie reminded him. "But, naw, you let him do it. And now, look at what's happening. You knew Keith was *dramafied.* Especially, when things don't go his way."

"Queenie, I didn't know he was like that. What was I to do??? He walked in while you were bent over on the balcony, and I was inside you."

"You should've said, *hell naw*," Queenie replied, easing off of the Reverend's erection, and exposing her well trimmed coochie. "That's my brother, and all, but he's always trying to run and take over any and every-thing. It's all about Keith."

"Then he would've got mad and began to run his mouth around the congregation," the Reverend shot back. "All I need is for Eva to find out about us." Rolling over on his side and looking to Queenie for advice, he said, "What do I do? Tell Keith to fall back, and satisfy Lawrence and Rita; or do I kick them out, and keep Keith so that I won't be in deep water with the Preacher's Conference Committee? I'm a public figure in the community. I can't afford to lose my reputation over a bunch of nonsense. Nor do I want to lose you."

"Well, you messed up getting rid of Doug and giving the spotlight to Keith." Queenie faced the Reverend and crossed her legs Indian style. "Because it's going to be Keith's way or no way." She ran her fingernails over his shiny bald head. "You don't have to worry about losing me. I'm in love with you, Earl."

"I thought that was the way you wanted it," he reasoned while cozying up to her gentle touch the way a cat would to its owner. "I need you to come to the rescue. I can't take a chance at losing our best musicians."

"No one moves a church like *Rita*."

"She can sang, can't she???"

Giggling, Queenie quickly replied, "Naw, you mean, *she sure can fill a church up*."

Reverend Reeves had a stoic look on his face. Queenie had read him real good. And he knew it.

"I didn't mean any harm by that, Earl. I just know she's an intricate piece to your peace. And at the same time, you know I'm going to keep it one hundred with you always." She leaned in for a kiss, trapped his bottom lip between her bite, then let go before saying, "I'm the mistress and all, but I do want you happy the same way a first lady would want you happy."

Queenie had no problem being number two in the Reverend's life. But the more he sought her advice and perspective on matters of life, the more the desire to have more with the Reverend escalated. The gifts were great, the intimacy was immaculate, but even a home-wrecker had visions of one day having a home.

"So, umm, any suggestions, Queenie?"

"From what Keith has told me, he's got some young lady coming by before rehearsal on Saturday. He claims she can blow like Yolanda Adams."

The Reverend sighed deeply. He then asked, "When did this all fall into place?"

"Well, I was reading a book by BOOG DENIRO, and he came in and interrupted me…"

"BOOG who?"

"DENIRO. This hot *street fiction* author from New York. He's written a lot of books. I googled him, and it turns out, he started his own company, with a sibling, from prison. He's been locked up since he was nineteen, almost twenty years, on a conspiracy case. From what I've read, sounds like he may've been wrongfully convicted. The DA got his *best friend* to lie on him. They used false testimony, and fabricated evidence. His best friend has since recanted, and another witness has emerged with information that was just introduced to the courts. He's got a lot of people signing all kinds of online petitions in his support and everything."

"BOOG DENIRO, huh? New York, hmm? Maybe Edward knows him. Edward's from the big city too."

"But, back to Keith. So, he comes in, running his games, and I told him…*Earl ain't going for that.*"

"That's something I think you should've told me right after he started talking that mess."

Raising her voice a bit, Queenie said, "I didn't want to get caught up in the middle of it! But you have my word, I will talk to him. He's supposed to be going to a hair show in Raleigh with some coworkers…"

"Good." The Revered rolled back over on his back and looked to the heavens. "We don't need chaos like this in the congregation."

Queenie loved when the Reverend needed her. And when he used the word *we.* Inclusion was an addiction of its own. She also loved when he looked at her like she was the finest woman in Durham. She figured it would only be a matter of time before he was filing for divorce. That was the *end game* right? For her to become the next *Mrs. Earl Reeves*? *With his rich ass*?

Although that had never been discussed.

Marjorie was on the Reverend's mind too. But that, he could discuss with no one. He couldn't believe she had tried to get him to get his boys to take a life for her own selfish greed. He wondered what else she was hiding, capable of, and that maybe that was why the offerings were light as of lately.

Queenie leaned in and kissed the Reverend. His cheek, his forehead, his lips, his nose, all while mounting him. She pulled her teddy up over her fresh hairdo and tossed it to the side. She had not stretchmark on her naked body. Gravity was still her homey, and it showed in her lush breasts. She put her full chest right in his face.

Lord, I need your guidance more now than ever.

Chapter 18

It was a Friday night, and DJ Shout was filling his slot on 88.1, as Marlo expected. Perfect for his party on wheels. He had been cruising the streets of Durham, accompanied by his new boo, and hoping that would get Tracey to loosen up some more. A lot of question marks still lingered around her.

Zaxby's was up ahead on Hillsborough Rd, so Marlo veered towards the drive-thru, even though he could see a line of cars moving at a snail's pace.

"I've never ate at Zaxby's," Tracey said in a low pitch, as he inched to the speaker.

"I know that feeling," he joked. "First time for everything. And I'm hoping for some *more firsts* tonight."

Tracey laughed that off. She knew exactly what Marlo was alluding to. His mind was extremely easy to read. Something she liked. "At least let me pay," she suggested, reaching into her D.K. purse for some cash.

"My treat."

When Marlo looked at her, a twenty dollar bill was between her fingers.

"No."

About a minute later and while Tracey was still holding the bill, Marlo ordered them two barbeque fillet chicken sandwiches with fries. "Tracey, what are you drinking?"

"Dr. Pepper."

"One large Dr. Pepper, one Coke," Marlo concluded the order with. He then took the twenty from Tracey's fingers and buried in her cleavage. Real nice and slowly. The way a man would do a sexy sistah at a gentleman's club. Tracey thought there was some attractive things about her, but she had never felt like a sexy sistah. She blushed and squeezed her thighs together, while trying to catch her breath, and unable to take her eyes off Marlo.

"What?" he asked, grinning.

"Can I ask you a question?"

"As long as I get to ask some of my own," Marlo replied licking his lips, further enticing Tracey.

Tracey got in a comfortable position. She propped her left leg up under her to brace herself for what she was about to say. "I notice that when we're together, your phone rings non-stop, until the point of you shutting it off." Before Marlo could reply, she further stated, "And you always have rolls of hundreds."

"Okay, and you question is?"

"Where do you work?"

A young Mexican girl, about 16-years old, stood in the pick-up window, chewing gum. She was holding their order waiting for Marlo to roll down his window.

"Yo!" the Mexican girl said.

Here she go again, all up in my damn business, Marlo thought as he let the power window.

Watching Marlo open the middle console between their seats, Tracey noticed more wads of money, all rubber-banded up. She turned her face the other way, and shook her head. He couldn't understand why.

Marlo paid for their food, then tipped the young Mexican girl with a $100. The young girl was ecstatic, and didn't take her eyes off of Marlo rimmed up vehicle until it was out of her periphery.

Tracey took the bags and checked them before saying, "Pull over right there." She directed Marlo towards an empty parking space off to the side of the restaurant. "Everything is there."

As he pulled into the vacant spot, Marlo put his car in park, let the motor run, and bobbed his head to the music. Tracey continued to ponder while Marlo began to flow with the song, "*When we came to the can*," by Boosie Bad Azz. Wanting to get back on the subject, Tracey said, "I was talking to you, mister."

Marlo continued to jam, as if he were in a studio.

"Marlo, we were talking," Tracey said, with stern eyes. She knew the deal, but wanted to hear what Marlo had to say for himself. If she were to save him from himself, he would have to face the music and admit he was dealing.

Marlo hit a button on the steering wheel and the volume was lowered. "Okay, I'm listening," he replied as he dug down in one of the bags between Tracey's legs. "I wish you would let me dig in something else."

"You need to stop," Tracey uttered holding back a blush. She liked his aggressiveness, but intervention was where her head was.

"*Shiiiit*, ... I'm dead serious," Marlo shot back as he bit into his sandwich.

Tracey snarled, while rolling her eyes, and out came, "I asked you a question. The money? What's up?"

"Look, Tracey," Marlo shot back with a mouthful of food. "Me, and my cousin, we have our own business. *Landscaping*."

"*Really*? Because, every time I turn around, you're either home, or just coming from somewhere. You two are never at work."

"We're the boss. The crew handles everything," he explained with barbeque sauce oozing from the corner of his mouth. Before Tracey could further interrogate, he washed the food down and said, "All we do is set up the contracts."

Tracey accepted that as true, and stared back out of the passenger window. She knew it was a lie.

"You don't believe me, huh?" he quizzed, reaching back into the bag between her legs for a few fries. "I know you don't. I'm no fool. So where do we go from here? Like, what's up???"

Tracey helplessly ran her fingers through her hair and said, "I think you're a dope boy."

Marlo almost choked on the fries that he'd just stuffed in his mouth. "You got me all wrong," he stammered, as he began to swallow his food. "I'm no way involved in the dope game."

To think that Marlo would admit to disobeying the law to a woman he'd just met was unrealistic. And Tracey knew she would have to accept that. Obviously, it wasn't something he was proud of, disowned, and would also deny to his death. "Why are you staring at me like that?" he asked, with a puzzled look on his face. "I'm keeping it real with you, babe. DAMN."

"You know what you do for a living. All I know is, I work at a bank and I don't have money like you."

"But you act like you don't believe me or something, Tracey. Anyway, it seems that you're getting uncomfo-rtable. I'm a just take you on to the crib."

Tracey didn't want the night to end, and especially without making progress. But she didn't persist.

"You've got the wrong impression about me," Marlo pressed on, while driving a bit erratically.

The lying was beginning to irk her even though she really liked Marlo; even more than him almost missing the **stop sign**.

"Oh yea, make sure you're home tomorrow around ten," he ordered, braking. "The delivery truck from *Rooms To Go* will be delivering your bedroom suit."

"Tracey couldn't believe what she'd just heard. All she could do was stutter, "Marlo you didn't have to."

"What's done is done," Marlo said, pulling up to a red light. "Just make sure that you're home."

"So, what are you going to do after you drop me off?" Tracey inquired. "It's only 9:30. I thought that we would've at least hung out a little later than this?"

"I'm going to drop you off first. Then I'm going to *Blue Chips* at the Hilton, get toasted, and crash there. I'll be too messed up to drive."

"I don't mind staying at the hotel with you," Tracey offered, while sticking some fries in her mouth. While savoring the flavor, she ran her free hand over Marlo's crotch. "Just remember, the delivery in the morning."

"You just read me like a movie script. Now you wanna spend the night with me???"

"That sounds about right," Tracey admitted. Getting Marlo to admit he was a dope boy wasn't likely, but getting him to love her down was.

"Girl, I'ma give it to you *so good*," he began, under the intense caress of Tracey' palm and fingers. "So good, you may start telling me things about yourself I shouldn't know."

$ $ $

While Marlo and Tracey were taking their connection to the next level, Sack was home entertaining Laverne. When Pokey vanished, Laverne reappeared. Sack had been down on himself. Not just because he was craving crack, but because he had allowed his addiction to almost cost him his freedom. When Laverne showed up, she was on. She had a gram of crack, cigarettes, and a fifth of gin. As Laverne sat on the couch and took a blast, Sack decided to share the details of the drama that almost erupted with Pokey.

"He was just laying up in my shit, like he owned it," Sack relayed, as smoke drifted from his nose and mouth. "I ran his ass up out my shit."

"You should've, from what Yvonne is putting out on the streets," Laverne replied as she laid her pipe down on the coffee table. "Because, ain't no way he got popped with damn near an eight ball and didn't get booked or nothing." She reached for the clear bottle of liquor. "Yvonne work the streets like I do. She solid. There's no reason for her to lie on Pokey—as long as she'd known him."

"That's the damn truth," Sack shot back as he watched Laverne pour herself a shot. "He be tricking with Yvonne and everything. Normally, when he come here, she's with him. On the real, I knew something wasn't right."

When Laverne or anybody showed up to turn Sack on, he always got his rocks off by talking shit. Just gossiping. It was just Sack's way of life. He didn't give a damn about Laverne or anyone else. Just as soon as their dope and liquor was gone, he put them out fast as lightening. That's something he wanted to change about himself.

Laverne stated, as she held her liquor, "Honestly, when I came through the door and saw him, I started to turn my ass around, and dip."

Sack spoke up quickly. "Well, I'm glad you didn't, baby." He then laid his pipe down and reached for a drink. "Because, I needed to hear that shit about Pokey." Sack didn't feel so bad anymore.

"You say you put him out?" Laverne asked with a slight giggle and sat her glass back down on the coffee table beside her pipe, lighter, and a few broken up beige pieced of rock.

"Hell yea! Threw his ass up out here," Sack bragged. "He got too comfortable. First of all, everybody who came through, he was smoking up they shit. They came to see *me!* I'm, the houseman. Then he laying all up on my couch, stinking. Talking about a job."

"What?" Laverne shot back, grinning. She knew exactly how to pump Sack up. And got a thrill out it.

"Plus, while I was sleep, he was sneaking his ass in the *refridgidare* making sandwiches and shit," Sack told her through swigs of his liquor. "What really took the cake was his phone ringing and he wouldn't answer it. I was trying to chill and watch *Gunsmoke.* Then he tried to talk junk to me about beating my ass in my crib."

"Sack, no he didn't. He must don't know you, huh?"

Listening to Laverne and also getting hype from the

liquor, Sack was further amped. "He knew the deal. Smoke was coming off that ass. He almost crashed."

"Anyway, I thought he worked for Reverend Reeves?" Laverne quizzed, as she held her glass. Waiting for a reply, she crossed one leg over the other, displaying her beautiful legs, accentuating her short black skirt. "He think nobody know where he be getting that good coke from. All Reverend Reeves do is hide behind Marlo and that other nephew of his."

Sack was stunned and almost choked on his drink when Laverne's words registered. They were layered with salt.

Then she asked Sack, as she snapped her fingers, trying to remember, "What's his damn name, the smart and fine one, who go with Felita fly ass?"

"Nu-Nu."

Reverend Reeves was Sack's friend. And he had never ever heard anyone talk that way about the Reverend.

"That's it! *Nu-Nu!* And his uncle got people all on TV passing out. Reverend Reeves can't fool me," she ranted.

Sack was beginning to see Laverne as a detriment, not an asset. Sack was beginning to see Laverne as a whore, not a coquette. He was high and inebriated, but he wasn't a fool. *Earl wouldn't take kindly to such banter*. And if it were true, why hadn't the Reverend chosen him. That's what was going through Sack's mind.

"Laverne, I've been knowing Earl all my life." Even though the Reverend had made it and he hadn't, and they never really communicated anymore, there was still a level of loyalty. And though Sack was an addict, there were some things he still valued. And true friendship was one.

"He tried getting me in his car," she mentioned to ease the tension she felt brewing. "Trying to be slick about it too, like he wanted to talk about the bible."

The Reverend could have just about any woman he wanted growing up, and now, thought Sack. *There is no way the Reverend was trying to seduce your ass*. But it had been true. It was one of those days when Laverne was detoxing and was glowing in a flowing dress. Nothing about her said—*smoker!*

Laverne stared out into La-La Land and remembered that night. What made her reject the Reverend was she had promised her son she would spend his sixteenth birthday with him.

Sack Considered getting hold of ole Earl. Not for a handout, but to warn him about what may not be rhetoric. But before he did, he decided to do some damage control. He didn't want Pokey in a grave, or Earl in a cell. "Thanks, but it's about time to wrap this up. Got places to be, things to do, peeps to see."

Laverne hiked her skirt down over her hips and left.

Chapter 19

SATURDAY MORNING…

It was 8:25 AM, and Keith was sitting at a glass ivory dining table for four, as the ceiling fan spun slow right about his fresh haircut. He was nursing a steamy cup of brewed coffee, having just risen for the day after a fun but busy night at the hair show. Coffee usually got him perked up and ready for the day. This was the day that he'd longed for. The day he would unleash Kissie on the Jubilee Baptist choir.

I can't wait to see that bitch's face this evening, he thought as he stirred a spoon of French vanilla into his cup. *She's going to be hot when I give her those walking papers. Hotter than my brew.*

While Keith sat plotting, Queenie just so happened to strut in. She was wearing a black silk robe by Victoria's Secret, over the teddy, and a pair of black silk bedroom shoes to match. Queenie's appearance was as if she was Meghan Markle, by the way she strolled in. *Rip the runway!* came to Keith's mind.

"Good morning, *Ms. It*," Keith taunted, as he sipped his coffee with his pinkie finger extended. "What are you doing up so damn early? You should be tired, the way Earl was over here laying hands on your ass."

A chuckle followed that made Queenie's eyes get narrow and scary. Keith said, "What? I smelled that cologne. It's strong, girl. Can't be missed."

"Keith, kiss my wide beautiful shapely ass," Queenie replied, as she passed by him, heading towards the kitchen. "It's too early in the morning for all that. Did you make enough coffee for two?"

Keith's chuckling slowed, as he said, "Well good morning to you too." He then took his eyes from Queenie and looked at their beautiful plants decorating the area dining area. He started to leave the table and go to their bar where he could be alone and continue his plotting. But instead he said, "Who pissed in your cornflakes this here morning?"

Queenie was in the kitchen preparing a cup of coffee, trying to figure out a way she could approach Keith about calling off the introduction of Kissie. She knew Reverend Reeves was really counting on her to come through, so she didn't want to disappoint him. Whenever she needed him, he was there for her. Like buying her a car straight off the lot. Whether it was clothes or bills, he had her back. Queenie wanted for nothing.

Keith put his focus now towards his sister, because for some reason she wasn't herself. So, he got up from the table, walked over to the opening of the wall, and looked at Queenie in the kitchen from the dining-room as she poured creamer in her cup.

"What in the hell is wrong with you this morning, sis?

When she didn't immediately respond, Keith leaned forward and propped both elbows in the sill of the wall opening. He studied his sister. He was surprised she wasn't scrambling some eggs. "The world must be about to stop, If you're greedy ass ain't trying to eat."

Queenie continued to stand, glaring out the window, while sipping her coffee. Keith hated the silent treatment, and loved attention. When he got the cold shoulder, it agitated him. Keith knew his sister always embraced his sense of humor, and funny way of showing affection to his only sibling. Something was terribly wrong, and he wanted to know what it was.

"Queenie, did Earl do something to you? Because if he did..."

And there it was, the levies had broke. Her back was still turned to Keith, but he felt the wrath. "No! But, why is Lawrence calling Earl's phone, telling him you're causing problems in the choir?!"

Keith's posture straightened up. "I ain't causing no problems. Rita just don't want to get with the program." Keith strutted back to the table where he had been seated and continued, saying, "Then once I check her, Lawrence wants to step in, and add his two cents. So their asses got to go. They making my job too hard."

Before responding, Queenie walked over to the wall's opening and looked Keith square in the eye. "Ay, you can't get rid of Lawrence. I told you, that's Earl's cousin. And Rita definitely ain't going nowhere."

"Says who?" Keith asked boldly. "Because, last I checked, I'm in charge of the choir. And I have you to thank for that, *big sis*."

"Wait a minute now," Queenie said, as she made her way out of the kitchen and into the dining area. "Earl don't need that drama in the congregation." She pulled out a chair. "None of us do, Keith."

"It's a lot of mess that goes on in his church," replied Keith, while giving Queenie a hard onceover, "that his ass shouldn't have going on up in there."

Queenie knew what Keith was talking about, so she plopped her plump backside down in the chair and said, "And I guess you're talking about me and Earl's relationship?"

Keith shook his head, then sat his cup down rather hard. "Do you need the *hooked on phonics* version?"

"Forget you, Keith," Queenie snapped, pointing at him. "Earl knew you would eventually go there."

"Ya damn right," Keith made clear. "He shoulda been man enough to come to me about it. When he needs his voice heard, it always comes from you."

Queenie sat at the table and felt a sense of rage about to overwhelm her usually peaceful nature. She knew how Keith was. But her loyalty for the Reverend demanded she stand up for him. The last thing she wanted was to be caught between blood and her man. Queenie decided that it was best to keep her composure, and approach Keith in a different manner.

"So, Keith, for me, can you please work things out with Lawrence and Rita?" she asked as calmly as possible. "Earl, really needs for you to do this for him too."

"Noooo! It is what it is," Keith blurted, as he walked out of the dining area and headed down the hallway. "I done told Kissie to be at rehearsal today. And that's it. If I change my mind, it could make me look weak."

Before he was out of Queenie's visual range, he turned back and added, "If Earl's ass wants to run his mouth to you about that, he should've told you about those fake ass Vera Wang pumps that he bought you from *True Fitness*."

"What, you hater?

"A girl I was at the show with last night told me she seen him in there." His voice carried throughout the condo, then he slammed his bedroom door.

Queenie sat at the table stunned. And then she stormed off to her walk-in closet, each step shaking the condo. "There is no way!"

Keith heard her seething remark and knew he had fucked up. "Nobody's gonna win this game," he said sadly.

Chapter 20

The Carolinas was experiencing overcast, which for some law enforcement provided the best opportunity to go incognito. Durham wasn't that big, and pretty much, everybody could recognize everybody. At least, if the person wanted to.

Officer Green had been working off the clock, and around the clock, as there was much at stake. He was a peculiar man. Very odd and curious when it came to people who didn't resemble him. Not just blacks, but everyone with a brown hue. Officer Green thought there was no good in them. He thought people of color should return to their countries. Officer Green was a huge fan of President Trump, and voted for the wall. But his racially driven perspective changed when he met Kendra Judd.

Kendra Judd was a brown skinned country girl from a small town in North Carolina, with a population of 4,000, called Apex. Being fresh out the Academy, she had been on the Durham Police force for only a year. The moment Officer Green laid his piercing blue orbs on Kendra, intrigue conquered his fears. He already had a patrol partner, but constantly thought of ways to get rid of him and fill the position with Kendra Judd. The Lieutenant continued to blow him off, and then Pokey happened.

This was actually the first time Kendra had gone undercover. It was dangerous, but Kendra had an aura that spelled *fearless*. And she was smart. The first time he heard Kendra speak, it was as if he was hearing wise words being quoted. Officer Green was amazed by her. Kendra's voice and vernacular was like that of Michelle Obama. Officer Green was mesmerized.

Often he had pondered asking Kendra out, nothing fancy, just fun. Wholesome fun. After this huge bust, and once the Reverend and his nephews were in handcuffs, he would pursue her. Officer Green wanted to bring down the entire Jubilee Baptist Church. And celebrate with Kendra Judd.

He was right outside the Hilton, just a few spots from Marlo's flashy vehicle. He'd been there for too many hours, and growing inpatient by the minute.

Any minute the sun would shine and break through the clouds, so Officer Green wrestled with the decision of leaving, or checking on his partner. He decided to approach the desk at the Hilton and flash his badge.

After a few shrewd words and some swift convincing, the half-baked fellow slid the cop a swipe card to the room Kendra was in. He knew without a warrant he wasn't obligated to do so, but with his record, the closest he was supposed to come to working there was mopping floors. Not around the personal information of the hotel guests.

Officer Green stalked off towards the stairway. He

took two and three at a time, showing how nimble he could be. In no time, he reached the third floor. It was quiet, just one maid moving about like she hadn't had her caffeine yet. He waited until she bent the corner with her cart, then he approached the door being led by his ear.

He couldn't hear anything, and the thought that Kendra was behind that door, subdued in some sort of way invaded his thoughts.

Officer Green knew that if she wasn't in danger, he could compromise the entire investigation. Yet, he found himself making a move he would come to regret.

Having let himself in, the first thing Officer Green noticed were empty champagne bottles. He could see that off the large mirror on the wall. Next, he took in a pile of discarded clothing. That stopped him in his tracks. But only for a moment. *Maybe this is the wrong room*, he reasoned. But curiosity caused his to continue his tiptoe into the spacious suite. Pink toenails were sticking out from beneath a large comforter, right next to two large brown feet he was certain could only belong to a man.

The two bodies began to stir beneath the covers. And almost at the very same time, two heads popped up.

But with their vision slightly impaired because they were just waking up, Officer Green was able to slip back out.

"Wrong room," Officer Green seethed, realizing the

guy at the desk had duped him. The pink toes actually belonged to a white working girl who'd carried her naked frame out into the hallway with the neck of a champagne bottle in her grasp. "Motherfucker!" she shouted as the bottle crashed into Officer Green's right calf causing him to stumble.

Meanwhile, on the level below, Marlo and his new lover were gathering their things. Having been tipped off by the desk clerk, they quickly washed the scent of sex from their flesh and got dressed.

Marlo could not understand why the police was on his heels, while Tracey became capacitated with guilt. She did her best to put her hair back in place, while Marlo spoke in secrecy on his iPhone.

Although, Officer Green was unable to locate his partner, the fact that he followed them to the Hilton remained. So he called her, while boarding the elevator.

She ignored the first call. But she couldn't ignore the second one, because Marlo grabbed her by the throat and said, "*Answer it.*"

"Marlo, you're hurting me…"

"No one knew I had this suite but you," he countered with while loosening his grip. "Who's calling you? The cops?"

"No—"

"Then answer it," he seethed right in her face.

"Hey, Jamie," she began, "why are you calling me so early in the morning?

"Are you okay? I've been out front since last night."

"I'm fine, a bit tired. But fine."

There was a pause, a long one, before, Officer Green said, "Okay." He could feel it in his veins, she wasn't her normal self, and wondered had she gone too deep undercover.

As soon as Tracey ended the call, and sat her phone down, Marlo released her neck. "Who's Jamie?"

Before she could even say anything, he said, "The fucking cops are at this hotel asking about me."

"You have nothing to worry about. You haven't committed any crimes, right?"

"Right!"

Tracey exhaled, then wrapped her arms around Marlo's lanky waist. "Everything's fine…"

$ $ $

ALSO THAT MORNING…

Way out on the outskirts of Durham, near the Granville County line, Marjorie hid out at the Best Western Hotel off of exit 237 of I-85. With only credit cards, two suitcases, and hygiene items, Marjorie sat and wrestled with the thought of leaving the rest of her worldly possessions behind. She couldn't believe the Reverend kicked her to the curb, as if she was nothing.

Especially after giving something to him so sacred as her body. And after several years of celibacy.

Quickly, right before her eyes, Marjorie's world came crashing down. *How could he treat me this way?* she thought as she lay across the flower printed comforter. It was burgundy and covering a king size bed. She was crying her eyes out. *After all that I've been through, he treats me like this???*

Marjorie was in a frantic state as if she'd done nothing to create the predicament she now faced. It had been her idea to get him of her husband. It had been her idea to sleep with another woman's husband. And it had been her own lapse of judgment to give Reverend Reeves the ammunition, by playing checkers with chess playing Earl.

Neither the television nor the radio could be heard. The curtains were shut tight. All Marjorie did was lay in the dark hotel room, listening to traffic go by on the highway while plotting. She wanted revenge.

"I can't let Earl play me like this," she seethed as tears mixed with eyeliner turned her cheeks black like the room. "He knows I need him now more than ever, and he turns his back on me???"

Marjorie began to shake uncontrollably. Rage led her hands to the headboard, and she shook that like a mad woman. The police showing up at her place had spooked her. And all the cop had asked was, "Were you aware that your husband was considering divorce?"

With that she panicked. No one could tell her an arrest warrant wasn't being drafted up for her right now. It was the guilt that had her tripping. And Reverend Reeves' rejection just added to it. In all actuality, the cops were just acting on a tip. And the Lieutenant decided to send regular cops instead of detectives, just to see how she would react. And since she was part of the Jubilee Baptists senior staff, they figured if there was any funny business, she could be helpful in the other investigation.

She began to pace. Then she kicked her shoes off, and trudged in her own agony.

Suddenly, a thought came to her mind. Joy began to surge through her body. Marjorie began to dry her eyes, as a plan came together in her mind. *Lord, please forgive me for my sins...and wrongdoing...past, present, and future...*

$ $ $

SATURDAY EVENING...

Reverend Reeves and Eva had been home occupying the loveseat in their living room. Even with him watching television and Eva on her phone with Gloria, they were able to enjoy each other's company. Eva thought the quality time was overdue. Suddenly, the Reverend heard his phone chirp on the end table beside him. Seeing that Eva was in deep conversation, he grabbed his phone and looked at the screen. It was the *411* from Queenie. Keith wasn't folding, Kissie would be at choir practice.

Reverend Reeves dropped looking at the game, kissed Eva on the cheek, and slipped out the back door. He hadn't even heard Eva ask where he was going. He needed speed to get through the busy traffic, so that he could somehow intervene and put a halt to Keith's madness. He only had an hour.

Quickly, he jumped into his Corvette and sped off with Eva watching from the back door which was all glass.

Upon arriving at the church, the Reverend noticed Lawrence and a few other choir members ambling around in the main foyer. Scoping out the vehicles, he was glad to see that Keith hadn't arrived yet. Reverend Reeves parked, jumped out his whip, slammed the door, and hurried inside.

As he entered, he noticed Lawrence, Rita, and Doug talking amongst one another. Even though Doug wasn't directing the choir anymore, he still came to unlock the church for the choir to have rehearsal.

Edward Haywood just so happened to be posting fliers on the church's information board when Reverend Reeves approached him and extended his hand. Edward noticed the Reverend was wearing another Rolex. This one was solid gold with a brilliant and bright bezel.

"Sky Dweller," Edward recognized.

Revered Reeves grinned. "Boy, you know your stuff, don't you?" He was proud to be him, and couldn't help but to sneak a peek at the new timepiece adorning him left wrist. *$20,000*, he thought.

Edward, on the other hand, had no doubts the final payment would follow that firm handshake. Then that chapter of his life would be closed. Strictly Edward Haywood; Eddie Caine was dead. Having given his life to the Lord, he was certain his past would have a hard time catching up with him.

Since arriving in Durham, not only had Edward enrolled his children in the best schools, but he had also taken some business classes at the Community college. While enriching his business acumen, he invested his money wisely. His marriage was thriving physically, mentally, and spiritually. Leaving New York turned out to be the best thing he could've done.

"Reverend, you look like a million bucks," Edward said, sizing Reverend Reeves up and smiling.

The Reverend replied, "That's it?"

Both men laughed, then Edward said, "You look like you got something on your mind. Talk to me, old head."

Smiling, the Reverend said, "I have something for you—in my chambers. If you would just follow me."

That was the final payment. But Edward knew the Reverend wasn't still smiling about the million bucks joke. He put the last thumb tack into the landscaping flier, which was next to his wife's interior decorating advertisement, then shut the glass enclosure and followed Reverend's signature stride.

Once inside the chambers, the Reverend slid Edward a Louis Vuitton duffel clean across the long table that was reminiscent to the one on the *Last Supper* painting anchored to the wall. "It's all there, Eddie Caine," the Reverend announced like he was some drug lord. "After you check it out; it's on to the next." He then retrieved an elaborate money machine for Edward to use, just to speed things up.

Edward had plans for that money. And counting it in the Lord's house wasn't part of the plan. So…he zipped the bag back up and grabbed it by the straps.

"Have I gained your trust that much, Ed?" the Reverend wanted to know, as he grinned cunningly.

"I do trust you, Earl. That's why we did what we did. And I'm so glad it is over."

"Edward, I need more product."

"When we started this, I told you—once the fifty kilos were gone. I am done. Didn't I?"

The Reverend was stunned.

It took three years to disperse of the coke Edward had packed into an unnoticeable RV. Thanks to the internet, Edward found Durham. A big drug seizure had been broadcasted, which led Edward to believe there was an opening for him in the town if he could link up with the right person. Never in a million years, did he think the

Reverend would be that person. Someone who wouldn't get hot, wouldn't spread his business, and understand the necessity for change. So to see the panic in Reverend Reeve's eyes startled Edward.

"What, wh-what do you mean, you're done?" the Reverend stammered.

"It's over. Bigger and better things await us, my brother." Edward was stern.

"But, but—people are depending on me!!!"

Edward had never seen Earl shout like that. It was almost a shrill. Earl was even seething as he eyed Edward. Had someone been walking by, they may've sent up a few deacons.

"It's all gone. Every gram, Earl."

"I need more…"

"What do you want me to do, Earl--?"

The Reverend was thinking quick, as he moved in a small circle a couple times. "Give me the connect, Ed…" the Reverend suggested.

It became evident—Earl wanted to be Edward. And Edward wouldn't have minded walking in the Reverend's shoes.

Edward said, "Okay—"

"Yessss!" Reverend Reeves sighed.

"—if you give me the church."

"What?"

"I'll give you the connect, if you hand over the keys to the church."

If ever there was a time the Reverend was at a loss for words...that was it. It took challenges like that to put things back in perspective…

Chapter 21

SATURDAY @ 3:01 PM

From his bedroom window, Nu-Nu peeped a late model Mazda truck driving rather fast through the quiet roadways of the Strawberry Hills. The rumbling of the old engine is what made him leave his lady's naked and stacked figure in bed.

Nu-Nu watched intently until the dusty bucket pulled up in front of the condo, wondering who in hell was behind the wheel and interrupting his alone time with his Nubian queen, Felita. He knew if he was disturbed by the noise, then surely his neighbors were too.

"Come back to bed, Nu-Nu," Felita urged in this tantalizing twang, while patting the spot he had been occupying before he high stepped to the windowsill and parted the curtains.

Nu-Nu was shirtless and holding a bottle of Johnson & Johnson baby oil. He was eyeing the truck down, but he wasn't really worried. Strawberry Hills had become his playground. He said, "Whoever is in that truck is just sitting there…like a damn weirdo, babe."

"Maybe he's lost."

When Nu-Nu didn't' say anything back, Felita said, "You need to come on back to bed, and finish what you started." She was laying on her flat stomach, with her round brown backside glistening from the oil Nu-Nu had been rubbing all over it.

Nu-Nu may've been masterminding the Strawberry Hills operation on behalf of his uncle, but Felita was calling the shots in their life. And she was growing impatient by the second. Felita rose from the silk sheets with her breasts bouncing as she flung her hair back over her shoulders.

The young and hot couple were supposed to be trying new things. Jaquees was playing in the background, setting the scene, and nothing was off limits.

Sack had been unable to get hold of the Reverend, and decided to visit the Jubilee Baptist Church. Half-way across town, he realized that was a bad idea, figuring Reverend Reeves was more than likely preparing to deliver Sunday's sermon. So he decided to go over and speak with Marlo or Nu-Nu. Nu-Nu preferably, since he remembered him being the one with the sense. And this was a sensitive matter.

Before exiting the truck, Sack sat and thought. He knew the can of worms he was about to open could lead to a lifetime scar for Pokey.

The Reeves' weren't known for being violent. They were known for being tight-knit, smooth, and as of recently...*dealers.* But loose lips have been known to bring *ungodly* behavior.

"Fuck it!" Sack blurted ou as he made his way up the walkway. "I gotta let these boys know what is being said."

Felita had corralled her man's manhood from behind with her lips on his ear. She caressed gently, taking his attention from the activity outside with the sexy move. Felita was a deadringer for *Atlanta Housewife* Porsha. Some had suggested, the only reason Nu-Nu had Felita was because he had all that money.

The slamming of the old truck's door startled Felita and Nu-Nu.

Sack took another deep sigh before pressing the doorbell. It looked more like the Nuclear Button and once he pressed it, there was no turning back.

Neighbors had also come to their windows when Sack's truck invaded Strawberry Hills, but all went back to their respected lives, having noticed who Sack was visiting.

The bell rang, and Nu-Nu and Felita were no longer startled, they were scrambling for suitable garments. Something they could throw on real quick.

Two minutes had gone by, and Felita was almost done squeezing her ass back into her *True Religion* jeans when Sack rang the bell again.

"Okay, okay—I'm ready," Felita announced having just pulled a tank top over her head and down over her juicy breasts.

Nu-Nu had on a wife beater, and a strap in his hand. Felita was licensed to carry. "It's old head Sack!" Nu-Nu revealed to Felita like she knew who he was talking about, and with his eye still in the peephole. "Take this back upstairs. I'll be a minute, babe."

When Nu-Nu was done taking off the deadbolt and the door was opened, Sack said, "I'm looking for Earl."

"Oh yeah," began Nu-Nu. "What for?"

"I've been calling him, and he won't answer. And I sure ain't driving out to Treyburn. Hell, I ain't making it pass security anyway."

"Yeah, that sounds about right. If he didn't answer his phone, maybe he just busy. When did you call?"

Sack pulled his Obama phone out and showed Nu-Nu the screen.

"Man, unk ain't had that number in years. That's why he ain't answering."

"That's my fault. I been under a rock, not him," Sack admitted, stuffing his phone back in his back pocket.

"It gotta be important for you to be coming out this way. What's up?" Nu-Nu stepped back and said, "Come in. Just remember, I'm in the midst of something. So make it quick."

While they talked, Sack couldn't help but notice how good the Reverend's nephews were living. Electronics that Sack couldn't even pronounce or turn on littered the place. At his crib, all Sack had was an old Emerson TV and a throwback JVC sound system that he got when was across seas in the Army. That was years ago. Sack seen that time had passed him by as he was getting high.

Now Nu-Nu was a man. He wasn't the young kid Sack recalled giving dollar bills to for penny candy. It was as if Nu-Nu was the adult now, because from what he heard from Laverne, Nu-Nu definitely had the candy Sack desired.

Sack asked, as he felt a since of comfort, "Do you mind if I have a seat?"

"No, no," Nu-Nu replied, as he extended his hand towards the couch. "You know, you're like family. Would you like a drink too?"

"Boy, you know you're unk, don't you?" Sack shot back, not realizing he didn't have to butter Nu-Nu up. "I could sure use one." From where he sat, Sack could see the Rum, champagne, Grey Goose, the Ciroc, and Hennessy. "Doesn't matter, you pour, I'll drink."

"Mr. Sack, you still got it, I pray when I get your age, I'm still as spunky."

"Aww, I ain't hitting on shit," Sack said as he watched Nu-Nu grab the Ciroc by the neck. He then took a gander at the photos on the wall. "Seeing you in all these pictures with that sexy babe, I want to be you."

Nu-Nu laughed as he stroll back to the living room with some Hennessy too. He handed Sack a glass and coaster. Though he was laughing a bit, and showing hospitality, Nu-Nu was dying to know why Sack's ass was sitting on his sofa. Nu-Nu knew the Reverend hadn't dealt with Sack in years. It wasn't because they were beefing or anything. Mainly, it was because in life, people just begin to do their own thing.

Nu-Nu poured Sack a nice drink, to the brim, then walked over and took a seat on the recliner directly across from him. As he was leaning back, he caught a glimpse of Felita out the corner of his eye, back in her birthday suit, and ready for some action. He knew he had to speed things up. "So, you said that you were trying to get in touch with unk. Why, and after all these years?"

As he held his premium liquor, Sack replied, "I need to see him." Then he downed it. "Is there any way that you can give me his new number?" Sack bemoaned as he sat the empty glass down on the coaster which sat on a glass coffee table. "I got to talk to him about something very, very important, that I heard."

There was no way he was giving Sack the number. No one got the number, not even the Mayor. And the Mayor once came to Jubilee Baptist Church to do a campaign speech for future votes.

"Nothing against you, but Uncle Earl would be pissed, if I gave you his number. Talk to me, what do you want? Why are you here?"

Sack began to think a little more than he wanted to. It was the liquor. He had drank too much and too fast. Nu-Nu knew what he was doing when he filled it to the top. And Sack was beginning to realize it too. The Reeves boys moved as one. He was about to start talking when Nu-Nu said, "What, do you need a loan?"

Before he could reply, Nu-Nu filled his glass up again, and motioned for Sack to drink. Sack drank, pretty much gulped it down. He could hold his liquor, but he couldn't hold his tongue.

Suddenly Sack said, "So, ahhh, when was the last time you seen or heard from Pokey?" A husky belch followed that.

"Been about a week," Nu-Nu replied, with a puzzled look on his face. "Believe it or not, me, my girl, and Marlo was just talking about that the other day. He normally takes the Land Rover to get detailed on Thursdays. Is he okay?"

Another burp came up out of Sack's body. "Well, yes, and no. I have some disturbing news, that Earl must know."

Nu-Nu saw that Sack was careful with his words. So he filled the glass again, and moved back into the recliner. This time he mixed the Ciroc and Henny.

Sack couldn't resist the strong drink. Especially since it was free. But he didn't down it. He sipped and began talking again. "Where is Ole Earl?"

For Nu-Nu to be his age, he was very sharp and mature. Once being an Honor student at Northern High, and also playing on the men basketball team, he earned a scholarship to Appalachian State. In his third year of college, along with Marlo, Nu-Nu was introduced to the dope game by his uncle. Since being on the road to the riches, college held very little relevance to Nu-Nu. Still, he was intelligent enough to entertain any conversation, whether it was street or intellectual. "Is Pokey hurt or something?" he inquired, watching Sack closely.

"Let me put it to you this way," Sack began with the spirits easing his nerves. He sat the glass down and spat, "From what I heard, Pokey was out Braggtown with a chick named Yvonne, getting high in his van, and the police ran up on his ass. Got him with a eight-ball."

"You bullshitting!" Nu-Nu shot back in disbelief, and wide eyed. "When was this?"

"From what I hear, about a week ago. This lady friend of mine, real nice legs, and a hella ass, like the lady in that picture right there." He pointed to nine-by-twelve, of Felita and Nu-Nu all hugged up. "Anyway, she told me this in front of Pokey."

"Hold up, so you seen Pokey?" Nu-Nu asked, with stress lines on his forehead. "Well, how did he get out?"

"He never went in, young man," Sack said, shaking his head from side to side. "The lady said, they let him go. No charges."

"They let him go?" Nu-Nu asked, sliding back in the recliner. "He must didn't have nothing on him."

"I just told ya, he had an eight-ball. That's the word on the streets, *family*. That's what I want to talk to Ole Earl about. He was hiding out at my crib..."

"No, fuck no. That's a damn lie. Nobody gets busted with an eight-ball and don't go to jail."

"Unless, they snitching," Sack slid in.

Nu-Nu wasn't with the slander. But when it came to people suffering from addiction, anything was possible. *If Pokey wasn't in jail, why hadn't he called or came around?* Nu-Nu wondered, and figured he'd better find out immediately.

"So, Mr. Sack, who is this lady that you're getting this so called info from?" Nu-Nu asked as he raised up out the recliner.

"Laverne, and she's at my house right now."

"Right now?"

Sack nodded confidently, as if he was in possession of the Nuclear Code. "That not it though. She's also saying your family is giving Pokey the coke."

"She said, what?" Nu-Nu stammered, all wide eyed.

While they sank deeper into the rabbit hole, Felita came out of the room again, this time with a sheet wrapped around her. "Bae, Marlo is on the phone right now." She tossed it over the railing just as Marlo hit his stride. "He says, it's important."

Nu-Nu knew that if Marlo called the crib and said that it's important, it meant either money or trouble. "Mr. Sack, excuse me for a minute," he sounded off, trotting towards the staircase just in time to catch the phone.

"Yo, cousin?" Nu-Nu quizzed while Felita stood watching him lovingly. "We'll talk more when you get here." With that, Nu-Nu hung up.

"What happened, Nu?" Felita asked, looking at Nu-Nu, as he held the phone, standing in a trance.

He whispered to Felita, "The police was at the front desk at the Hilton asking questions about Marlo." Then he looked over at Sack. "Take me to your crib, Mr. Sack. I need to have a word with this so-called friend of yours..."

Chapter 22

Back at Jubilee Baptist, Reverend Reeves and Edward was in the midst of a hostile environment. Keith had showed up with Kissie. As soon as he came through the door, drama began. While Reverend Reeves stood between Keith and Lawrence, Edward kept Rita back from Kissie. The rest of the choir stood back and watched along with the musicians. It was as if a tag-team match was about to transpire.

The Reverend couldn't believe how ego-driven Keith was. Queenie had been right. In his mind of minds he was trying to come up with a quick solution to resolve the problem. "Keith! Keith—for me," the Reverend begged, as he held Lawrence back. "Let's handle this the right way."

Keith continued to throw a tantrum as if he wanted to get to Lawrence. "Naw, Earl, I want them up out of here!" he blurted out. "I'm tired of him and *her*. They gots to go. Kissie, is the new leader of the choir."

Lawrence wasn't saying nothing at all. He'd been waiting for the perfect time to smash Keith. Right at that moment, he didn't care. It was about to go down in the house of the Lord. Lawrence had decided to punch Keith in the mouth. It was like he was back on the prison yard.

Edward was struggling to hold Rita back. Kissie wasn't trying to burst a grape. All she knew was Keith had done got her caught up in some chaos that she wasn't expecting. Looking at Rita's full figure, she was glad that the Reverend and Edward was there to meditate, because a beat down would've definitely came her way.

Edward got tired of holding Rita back. His mind worked a lot faster than Reverend Reeves'. Having spent time in recording studios back in New York, Edward came up with a plan. *Hell...yeah,* he thought. Then he bassed verbally, "Hold up! *Hold up!*"

Hearing Edward shout like an authoritarian, everybody calmed down. They had never heard Edward raise his voice before. Even the choir, Doug, and the musicians gave him their full undivided attention, as if they were involved.

Reverend Reeves was glad that the drama was at cease for minute. The adrenaline rush caused him to break out in a sweat. The only time the Reverend cared to sweat was either, preaching or having sex. Besides hearing about the dope connect being a wrap, he thanked God for allowing Edward to be there to help him out. It was very much needed. *Soooo necessary.*

"So, is this how Christians act???" Edward asked, as he looked around at everybody. Edward only stood at 5'4", but it felt as if everyone was looking up to him. *Except Keith.*

Shifting his weight from one foot to the other, hands on his hips, Keith rolled his eyes. Even though he didn't want to hear it, he knew Edward was right.

"Maybe I joined the wrong church," Edward stated, as he then looked from Rita to Lawrence. "Because I can find this action in the streets, where I used to be twenty-four seven."

Reverend Reeves couldn't do anything but look down at the teal blue carpet. He was convicted due to the sincerity in Edward's voice. Jubilee Baptist wasn't as holy as it should've been. And it all started with him. By the Reverend being the watchman that God spoke of in the book of Ezekiel Chapter 33 verse 6:

But if the watchman sees the sword coming and does not blow the trumpet to warn the people and the sword comes and takes someone's life, that person's life will be taken because of their sins, but I will hold the watchman accountable for their blood.

He knew deep down inside it was darkness in the church, and he needed to clean house. Edward's voice was that *mighty sound* of the trumpet and it caused the watchman of the congregation, which was Reverend Reeves, to get his house in order. "So, Edward, in this situation, what do you feel that I should do?" he asked in a calmed tone, and in front of everyone.

Everyone could see Reverend Reeves valued Edward's opinion greatly. Edward turned to Keith, then to Kissie. Next, he checked out Rita. After hearing all that Edward stated, Lawrence began to walk back and take his position with the rest of the musicians. He also un-balled his fists.

"You, Doug," Edward barked, as he turned towards him, "come and stand beside Rita."

With a puzzled look, Doug looked around as he was lost and made his way to Rita's side.

Reverend Reeves stood beside Keith, and Kissie on his left with a curious look on her face. "Edward, what is going on?" he inquired, crossing his arms over his chest, his Rolex gleaming.

Edward continued to stand with Keith and Kissie on his left, while Rita and Doug posted up on the right side of him. "Reverend Reeves, I say we have a *sing off*," he revealed, as he stood in his Neiman Marcus blue jeans and white Tee. Not only did Edward have on a pair of white-on-white *Foam Posit* Air Force Ones, but he was iced out from his neck to his fingers. It was Saturday, and Edward just wore something loose and comfortable to go out and hang fliers in.

"A sing off?" Reverend Reeves shot back, with an interested gleam in his eyes. "What do yo mean?"

Quickly, Edward began to explain, "It's simple. If Keith wants this lady to take Rita's position, she's gonna have to take it with her God given talents."

Then Edward added, "Put it like this; if she wins Rita loses her spot. If Rita wins, Keith's friend is not in the choir, Keith is out, and Doug gets his spot back. That's what I feel is the best solution to this madness."

Reverend Reeves could not hold back the smile that began to dominate his handsome face. He knew that God had to have orchestrated this master plan.

"Let's do this thang!" Keith taunted loudly, as he laughed with confidence in Kissie. "*Ms. Thang*, you might as well get to stepping now."

Rita brushed the comment off. Like, literally. The way Jay-Z had dusted that dirt off his shoulders. Edward was smart. He had faith in Rita. Anytime someone can sing and move him, there is potential to be a star. Edward had hung out with many singers in his past. Rita was one that he also kept his eyes on. Making music was really his first passion, not dealing drugs.

"Rita, it seems that Keith and this young lady is all in," Reverend Reeves stated, as he looked at her and Doug. "Are you two all in?"

Rita took a long look around the church. She thought about the repercussions of her decision if she were to lose. Rita remembered day one when she joined Jubilee Baptist. All the counseling that Reverend Reeves had with her. She could even hear past performances in her mind from years ago. Also, she thought about how not being in the choir anymore could interfere with what she and Lawrence were building. She had even began to see results from their daily trips to the gym. If Rita were to be defeated, she would have to see Lawrence from the pews, and may never perform with him again. Still, she looked at Doug, Edward, and Reverend Reeves, and said, “Let’s do this.”

The choir and musicians looked at one another. In the choir, they’d never had a sing off for a position. This was something new and innovative, thanks to Edward. Everyone braced themselves for the battle. And the future of the choir.

While everyone stood and watched, Doug went and got two microphones. He handed one to Kissie, who looked stunning, and the other to the confident Rita.

Watching intently, Reverend Reeves knew that sacrificing Rita to conceal his sins would be a hard pill to swallow. He lowered his hazy gaze and said a silent prayer on Rita’s behalf. Even said one for Kissie. When he looked up, he noticed that Queenie had arrived. And then out the corner of his eye, he saw the First Lady.

Who in the name of God called these women? he wondered as his armpits began to experience wetness.

There was so much going on that he was able to get over to Eva’s side, and say, “What are you doing here?”

Eva whispered back, “I got a call, there might be some trouble with the choir?”

“Really?”

“That’s what I said. I just wanted to be here to support you.”

The Reverend sighed, then said, “Everything is fine. You can go on home, my dear.”

The crowd seemed to be growing, and Eva had to raise up on her toes to see into the center of the crowd.

"Are you sure, everything is fine, Earl?"

"I am positive."

Eva asked him to walk her to her car, and he did. When he came back through the church's doors, Queenie was hiding in a secluded hall. She snatched him by his sleeve and yanked him into the shadows where she planted a huge kiss on his unsuspecting lips.

"I heard you decided to have a sing off," she said, rubbing her fingernails all over his chest.

"I, I—" the Reverend began, then thought better. "I can't take credit for the idea. It was all Edward's idea."

The Reverend kissed Queenie back, palmed a soft behind a bit, then said, "I have to get back. This could be the very last time I see Rita perform here." He took a few steps with Queenie not far behind, then turned back and asked, "How did you hear about the sing off so fast?"

"I got an anonymous text," Queenie replied, grinning. This was by far the most exciting thing to happen in her life in a long time. And her brother was right in the middle of it all. She didn't even ask the Reverend about the fake shoes. She would save that for another time.

Edward stood in the middle, looked at Kissie, and asked, "Are you ready to be the next leader--?"

Kissie was in a daze. She was checking Edward out from head to toe. The battle was the last thing on her mind. Edward looked even better in person. She had only seen him driving his Range Rover, and then his Bugatti around town.

"—of the choir? Excuse me, miss?" Edward added.

"It's Kissie," Keith said all loud, hoping she would snap out of the awestruck trance.

Edward reminded her of Floyd Money Maywether. She extended her hand for his, and said, "I am ready."

Reverend Reeves butted in, not noticing that he had lip gloss on his mouth. It was a good thing that the First Lady had been wearing the same *Mac Glass* brand. He said, "What song are you singing?"

Kissie replied, "Open Up My Heart, by Yolanda Adams, Reverend Reeves."

She took a deep breath, looked at Edward one last time, thinking of how fine of a specimen he was, then gave the signal for the musicians to crank up. They could pretty much play anything. Kissie revved up like a foreign car, and took off. Everyone's eyes stretched as Kissie sang. Keith had been right; Kissie sounded just like Yolanda Adams.

Reverend Reeves was into Kissie's performance. He was standing in awe with his mouth agape. Kissie could definitely blow. And he couldn't help but wonder what it was going to be like without Rita around.

Meanwhile, Keith was face fighting with Rita. It was as if he was saying, *See ya, woulnd't wanna be ya!*

Rita just ignored him and his childish antics. Instead, she gave Kissie praise for having such an amazing voice. And for looking like a star. She had to admit, the choir would be in good hands if she were to lose.

Once Kissie's performance came to an end, everyone applauded. There were even whistles. Rita felt betrayed. Edward raised hand to stop the clapping.

No matter what, Rita wasn't about to accept defeat. She put on a brave front, searched the crowd for Lawrence's eyes, which weren't hard to find, and then praised the Lord.

Kissie reached out for Edward's hand again, and everyone could see that she was into him. Keith grabbed her arm, and pulled her to his side, so that Rita could hurry up and get to losing.

Holding the microphone with confidence, Rita said, "Choir, stand to your feet."

Edward then inquired of Rita, "Have you chosen a song, Rita?"

Rita looked around one last time, then said, "I'm going to be singing *Work it Out,* by Vickie Winans. Choir are you ready?

Suddenly, Lawrence began to play the drums. The rest of the musicians fell right in with him.

"Choir, what will Jesus do?" Rita asked into the microphone.

The choir sang back: "*Work-it-out!*"

Rita sang, "Jesus will work it out!!!"

"*Work it out!*"

Rita sang, "I'll never have a doubt!"

"*Work it out!*"

Rita sang, "Jesus will work it out!!!"

"*Work it out!*"

Rita sang, "Baby…need a new pair of shoe!!!"

"*Work it out!*"

Rita sang, "Plus…I got a light bill due!"

It was like this incredible rendition would never end.

And nobody wanted it to.

Rita was perspiring, trembling, and laying it all on the line. She had regained her stronghold.

Reverend Reeves and Edward stood in amazement. Once again, Rita was blowing the roof off the church. Keith and Kissie knew just that fast, it was over. Doug made his way up to the choir and took his normal position in the director's spot. Lawrence puckered up his lips, and kissed the air towards Rita. When he did that, Rita got hyped and worked her way over to Keith and Kissie. She raised the roof even higher. Everyone knew Rita had defeated Kissie. And Kissie didn't need to hear it.

Keith was pissed. Quickly, he grabbed Kissie's wrist, as if she were a child in his care, and stormed off towards the main entrance where he had parked his car. That spot was no longer reserved for him.

A sigh of relief came over Queenie. But she had this feeling that they wouldn't be hearing the last of Keith.

The Reverend whispered into Edward's ear, "You are not just a brother in faith, you are a savior my brother."

Edward was really blushing now. He felt right at home. "Thank you. That means a great deal."

Reverend Reeves was cheesing, until Edward said, "You might wanna get that lip gloss off your mouth, before you get home to the misses…"

Subconsciously, the Reverend's right hand ascended to his mouth. "Thanks," he said, wondering if Edward knew that all this madness was the result of his infidelity.

Chapter 23

Nu-Nu slipped out of his Nike slides and into some Jordans, after talking to Marlo. Felita got dressed too and followed Nu-Nu to his Land Rover. "Babe, you can't go," he said, staring her right in the eye.

She was still moist between the legs, and wanted to be around her man, no matter what. She also sensed trouble. Nu-Nu tongue kissed her real good, then whispered, "I won't be long."

"Okay," Felita replied before ambling back to the condo. Normally, she would have put up a fight.

Nu-Nu took one last look at that ass, then followed Sack. Nu-Nu didn't like the fact that family dirt was all out in the streets. All he wanted was to see who this heifer Laverne was and get things straight. As he drove down Duke Lane, his phone rang through the speakers of his whip. Seeing the screen of the caller ID on the dash, Nu-Nu noticed that it was his uncle. He thought that maybe Felita or Marlo had called the Reverend and gave him the rundown.

On the second ring, Nu-Nu pressed the call accept button on the steering wheel and answered, "Hey, *unc*?"

"What's up, nep? I'm just calling to check on my favorite nephews."

"We're your only nephews."

"I know. Sometimes I just feel so blessed to have you

guys. Being as though, me and ya auntie Eva were unable to have kids."

"I appreciate that, unc."

"No really. Sometimes, I think about that. And my lower self wonders about getting a woman who can bear children to make me a father. Then I see you and Marlo, and I say to myself, *the Lord has already blessed me.*"

Nu-Nu was certain his uncle knew nothing about Sack and Pokey, or Marlo and the police showing up at the hotel, and he wasn't going to spoil the moment by telling him. He would handle it all. "Unc, is there anything else on your mind, because I have some things to attend to."

"No, no. That's it."

"Okay. What's all that noise in the background?"

The Reverend was still at the church, and they were still celebrating Rita's victory. He told Nu-Nu, "I'm in the Lord's house. And it was a beautiful day today. We'll talk more when we meet up, nep."

And like that, they were back in their own temporary worlds. Feeling relieved, Nu-Nu continued to tail Sack. In no time, they were speeding past Braggtown Projects. Sack's muffler was smoking; that made him think about Pokey and question why he didn't just tell the Reverend what was going on. He contemplated calling his uncle, and just telling him what Sack had conveyed, but nixed the idea. But for some reason, the Reverend called back, and when Nu-Nu answered, the Reverend said, "Have you heard from Pokey?"

As Nu-Nu continued to follow Sack, he said, "An old

friend of yours by the name of Sack, stopped by the condo today."

Reverend Reeves was puzzled, and Nu-Nu pictured the expression that might be commandeering his uncle's face. "So what does Sack have to do with Pokey?" the Reverend finally asked.

"He's saying Pokey ain't right."

"After all these years, he's still jealous of Pokey. So, he comes with some jive like that. Nep, when you winning, people are going to hate. You just have to let them hate. And with that, there is no better time, than now."

"For what?"

"That's what I wanted to talk to you and Marlo about," the Reverend stressed.

Before explaining, Reverend Reeves thought back to his days as a young man on the streets of Durham. Eva's sister and Pokey at prom came to mind, and Sack lurking in the shadows all upset that he was left out. He also recalled he trip to Disney World, -- Eva, her sister, the Reverend and Pokey. Of course, this was all before the drugs took hold of Pokey. Once again, Sack had been left out, and to exact revenge, he enlisted. Fastforward thirtysomething years, and Sack still was holding a grudge. Or so the Reverend thought.

"Nep, don't believe anything Sack says. You've been knowing Pokey all your life. Sack's an old school chum, but he's got a lot mess with him."

His word was platinum with Nu-Nu, and he knew that, so there was really nothing else to say.

Marlo, on the other hand, was all business. That kind of news from Sack would've made Marlo smoke Sack, Laverne, and Pokey, and ask questions later.

The Reverend said, "All Sack wants is a hit. Give him some money, and kick him to the curb."

"Gotcha, unc," Nu-Nu shot back then the line went dead.

Not long after that call, Nu-Nu was pulling over. Sack got out his truck and headed towards the driver's side window of Nu-Nu's Range. "Come on, nephew." Sack bassed in a drunken stupor. "The broad is in here."

Nu-Nu looked around at Sack's unkempt lawn and rundown brick house. Digging in his pocket, he pulled out a roll of money, and peeled off a Benji.

"Yo, Mister Sack," he sounded off handing him the money. "My girl just called. I've got to get going. If you will, take care of the lady for me. You know that we're not into the dope game."

"I know, nep," Sack slurred, making Nu-Nu wonder how in hell did he not cause a collision on the roads. He slipped the crispy c-note from Nu-Nu fingers and said, "Look, I'm about to go in here and straighten her out. She'll get her act right."

"Handle that for me, unc," Nu-Nu reiterated while holding back his laughter. Sack was twisted. "In fact, here's some more money. That's for her lying on Pokey." He gave him two more c-notes.

"Oh hell yeah, her ass is mine. Nu-Nu, what do you tell a broad who got two black eyes?

Curiosity made Nu-Nu stop the Rover from reversing

and ask, "What do you tell them?"

"You don't tell them shit. Because...you don't told them twice," Sack shot back, and then staggered off.

Nu-Nu was against domestic violence, had never laid a hand on a woman, other than to caress her. But he wasn't about to stop Sack from silencing the noise.

With that out the way, his mind went to what the Reverend needed to tell him and Marlo. And then, the cops inquiring about Marlo.

$ $ $

Inside the house, Sack straightened himself up. He wasn't as wasted as Nu-Nu thought he was. It was all an act. And he certainly didn't want Laverne to see him acting like a fool.

And not for one minute did Sack believe Nu-Nu. Laverne was his true friend, and the onetime beauty had been given great credence.

Sack was no fool. And he now had $300 to confirm that his old buddy was in fact a cocaine boss. People weren't giving out money for nothing. *Were they?*

Laverne was in his bed, grinning when he got there. Naked and ready to rock Sack's world. Her breasts were sitting up and slightly to the side. Her nipples were erect from the frosty air conditioning in his bedroom. And Sack was loving what he saw. Never before had he wanted Laverne as much as he wanted her that day. He could actually afford to take her off the track, if his moves were well calculated.

"You look like a very happy man," she told Sack.

I got a down payment on my future, Sack mused as he eyed Laverne's neatly trimmed pelvic area. *To keep me quiet, those Reeves boys are gonna have to pay me handsomely.*

"You ready for old Sack, girlie?"

"I sure is," Laverne said, snickering.

Sack sat the money on his end table, took Laverne's breasts into his hands, and kissed them like they were good luck.

Chapter 24

Tears began to cascade down Tracey's cheeks, and then came uncontrollable sobs. Marlo hoped she wasn't crying because he slapped a tight grip on her neck. He began to pace the bathroom floor uncertain of what to do. She wouldn't say anything, and he didn't exactly get known for consoling women.

"Tracey, I'm sorry," Marlo professed. He wasn't good at apologizing either.

"I'm sorry too," she cried.

"What for?" Marlo quizzed, now leaning over her shoulder awaiting Tracey's reply.

She had been stingy with the sex back at the Hilton, getting Marlo extremely worked up with those French kisses, only to pull away when he tried to get her out her sexy underclothes.

"For not letting me sex you?" he followed up with, wrapping his arms around her. "You gave me blue balls, but I'll get over it."

Tracey had been celibate for three years, although she had almost caved when Marlo slid his tongue up under the crotch of her panties, right where her butt crack and lady slit almost converged. If felt so good to her.

"I tried to help," she said sniffling.

"No you didn't," Marlo said, backing away from her, "but it's all good. There will come a day when you want this joy stick, kissing and licking all over it, and I'm gonna push you away."

Tracey laughed, said, "You are silly."

Marlo was relieved.

$ $ $

On the other side of that door, out and about in the condo, Fellita was cleaning house. Anywhere she saw something that resembled powder, she dusted and wiped down thoroughly. Not that they were sloppy or reckless, but she'd rather be safe than sorry.

After doing the entire first landing, she headed up the stairs where she would immediately hear sobs.

Felita put her ear to the door, not sure why, and posted up with the rag in one hand and some Windex in the other. She heard Marlo say something witty, then Tracey responded with light laughter, and then a minute passed with nothing.

Felita thought maybe they were having kinky sex—the kind that made a chick laugh and cry. She had experienced her share or joy and pain with Nu-Nu.

Just as she was about to walk off, she heard Tracey say, "*Marlo, I'm a cop.*"

Felita began to pace wildly, her lips curled into a wicked snarl. "I knew something was funny about that heifer!" she seethed through her tight lips and clenched teeth.

$ $ $

Meanwhile, instead of returning back to the condo, Nu-Nu went through the projects. Though, he respected his uncle's call, something about Sack and his woman friend's revelations rang as true. Nu-Nu knew his uncle could be biased when it came to family, and old friends. If he could speak to Pokey himself, Nu-Nu would feel a whole lot better.

The lights were bright in the projects at this time of night, and mostly trappers and addicts were out. It was easy for Nu-Nu to observe things. Most of the young trappers out that way weren't fond of Nu-Nu. They thought of him as a dude with a silver spoon in his mouth. A niggah who got lucky. Everything had been given to him. But his girl, Felita, she was not only beloved and respected in the hood, but she was known for having a temper too. So most people stayed clear of her ass.

The window on the Land Rover came down, as Nu-Nu pulled up on some young bangers in desperate need of some guidance. "Anybody see Pokey?" Nu-Nu asked no one in particular.

Everyone out there knew who Nu-Nu was, but no one answered him. They just glared. Nu-Nu wasn't the kind of hustler the young revered, or relished, whom would one day become a legend if he were killed or locked away in some state pen. But one kid saw a come up. He said, "He's over on the other side, by Slim's crib. I'll show you."

$ $ $

Marlo's mind began to race at the speed of light, as his whole life flashed before him. He hadn't completely succumb to the magnitude of what the woman staring him in the eyes had said, until he fell to his knees. *More like crumbled.* He expected her to pull her damn shield and read him his rights before slapping the cuffs on him.

"What the fuck?!" he wailed, scrambling to find his phone. "Fuck, fuck, fuck!"

"Calm down, Marlo," Tracey begged as she knelt next to him, putting her hand on his shoulder.

"WHY?" Marlo shouted. All he began to think was, *what the Reverend would think of him.* How he would never redeem himself. The female Donnie Brasco had infiltrated their organization…all because of him.

$ $ $

Inside the Land Rover, the youngster gave directions. Nu-Nu didn't like how the youngster kept reaching in his jacket pocket. As he drove, the young boy was also pointing, and Nu-Nu began to think it was a tactic to distract him.

"Take the left," the young boy directed, leaning against the passenger door.

"How do you know Pokey's up in Slim's joint?"

"Why you looking for a man who don't wanna be found?" The young kid was soft spoken and there wasn't much gust behind his words, yet they were deliberate.

Nu-Nu made the left without taking his eye off of the

young boy. "It's obvious huh?"

"I mean, the word is out, that he getting that rock off the Reeves boys," the youngster said, without hesitation.

Nu-Nu slammed on the brakes when he saw the young boy's hand slip from his pocket. He then threw it in park, and lunged over the console, attempting to subdue the kid. Nu-Nu wasn't much bigger than him, as far as poundage, but he was much smarter, and in survival mode.

The kid put up no resistance, just raised his palms to the sky like he was praising the Lord. "Yo, it's only my inhaler. I have asthma, big brah…"

A sigh of relief came over Nu-Nu, as he thought he was about to be attacked. "Shorty, I was about to do you, maaaan. No joke!"

"Slim's crib is right there," he assured Nu-Nu, while straightening up his clothes. "I saw Pokey in there about an hour ago. And my bad."

"What do you want?"

"I want off the streets. I was hoping you could introduce me to your uncle. I wanna be saved."

Nu-Nu couldn't believe his ears.

$ $ $

"Calm down, Marlo," Tracey begged. She truly dreaded this day. But if there was indeed a future for them, she would have to reveal her true identity. And, anticipate resistance from the guy she had fallen for. As well as rejection from him.

The good thing was, *Marlo had never committed a crime in her presence. Well, except exceeding the speed limit. But that was about it. No drug buys, no drug sales. No toting of the guns.*

Marlo was fidgeting with his phone when those things began to register with him. He took his eyes from his phone screen to glare at Tracey, and found her stepping out of her clothes. Her gun, her wedge shoes, her jeans, and panties, then her blouse and bra. She looked amazing.

"What are you doing, Tracey???" Marlo questioned, unable to take his eyes off her.

"Just wanted you to see, I'm not wired," she told him, reaching for the knob to activate a warm shower. "And it's *Kindra Judd.* Tracey is a fictitious name..."

Marlo immediately googled *Kindra Judd.* And all her info began to pop up. While he explored her public info, she began untying his sneakers. He didn't even realize Kindra Judd had successfully stripped him down to his boxer-briefs.

Not in Marlo's wildest dreams did he ever think he would be dating a cop. "Did you call the cops to the hotel, Trac—I mean, Kindra???"

"I swear on my dead daddy, I didn't," she asserted. "And I stripped down so you could see, I'm not wired or anything. I don't want to bring you down."

A fucking cop! Marlo marveled. *This is some movie shit!*

"Lift your arms up, "Kindra instructed Marlo, so she

could take his shirt off. Now they were standing right before each other. "I'm gonna take these off too..." She slowly slipped her fingers under the elastic and smoothly slid his boxer-briefs down over his hips and down pass his legs, grazing his manhood with her soft and smooth face. It tickled Marlo, sending some chills through his entire body.

"I read all your public information," Marlo said sitting his phone atop the marble finished countertop surrounding the large sink. The hot water was beginning to fill the bathroom with steam, further easing the mood, or one would say—*setting the tone.*

Kindra got close, so close Marlo's penis was on her stomach, facing upward, and almost reaching her cleavage. She said, "I want you now, Marlo. *You're mines!*"

$ $ $

Felita was still *ear hustling*, but she couldn't hear anything. She needed to make sure she heard what she thought she heard, before she could call her man and tell him what she thought she heard. A coat of sweat began to cover Felita's flesh as she waited to hear something. Anything. Finally, she heard her phone and Nu-Nu's ringtone.

Felita headed to the master bed, and quickly answered. "Hey handsome, where are you?"

"I found Pokey, babe."

Felita said, "Oh—"

"And we had a long talk."

"Oh—"

"He's going to rehab."

"Oh...where are you, I asked?" Felita said as she laid back in the plush California King bed and crossed her right leg over the left. "On your way home, I hope?"

"I'll be home soon. Gotta figure one more thing out."

Felita hung up on Nu-Nu.

With the youngster in the passenger seat and Pokey in the back, Nu-Nu looked on dumbfounded. Then his phone began buzzing. When he accepted, Felita's face appeared. She said, "I wanted to see you. *Marlo and his bitch is here*. And I miss you."

The youngster looked into Nu-Nu's iPhone, said, "Your girl looks better in person. I see her on Instagram and she be killing it on there."

Felita said, "Thank you, young man," as if she really needed anymore compliments. Her head was big enough. "He's cute, Nu-Nu."

"Well, that settles that," Nu-Nu exclaimed. He had wanted to see what Felita thought about the young fellow before just popping up with the kid.

A few minutes had passed by with the couple just exchanging thoughts, as Nu-Nu wheeled towards a local rehab clinic his uncle had worked with in the past.

Pokey was sleep, having not slept in days. And he was glad to be rescued. No one would be able to find him at the rehab.

The youngster turned up the stereo a bit to drown out the loud snoring, and Felita took that as a signal to end their *face-time* session. As she did, a knock was bestowed upon the double doors. Felita inhaled, exhaled, then said, “Come in!”

Marlo had his right arm draped over Kindra, and they both were wrapped in custom burgundy towels. Kindra’s skin was glowing, like she’d been exfoliating. Marlo was smiling like he had just conquered the world. And Felita began second guessing what she thought she heard.

“So what’s up?” Felita quizzed them both. “Don’t both speak at the same time. I know you’re not in my room for no reason.” She hadn’t even given them a chance to speak.

“Your room?” Marlo said, snickering.

“Nu-Nu is mine, so what is his is mine. And what is mine is his,” Felita recited like it was practiced of planned. She was eyeing Kindra pretty fiercely. So Kindra spoke first.

“...I know there is no easy way to say this, but—“

“But what?” Felita asked Kindra Judd.

“Let me talk first, Felita!” Marlo insisted.

“Talk!” Felita snapped, this time standing and placing her iPhone on the wooden bureau.

“My name is not Tracey, it’s—Kindra Judd. I work for the Durham Police Force. And I’ve been undercover for several weeks now...”

Felita’s foot, which was bare, tapped rapidly, as her eyes bounced back and forth between Marlo and *the bitch* Kindra Judd.

“I learned a lot over the last few weeks.”

"And what exactly is that?" Felita begged to know.

"That you guys are not hardened criminals, destroying the community, just a family who loves each other deeply. That's what I learned."

"Oh—"

Kindra Judd cut Felita off to add, "And I have reported such."

"—really?"

Marlo said, "Tell her the most important part."

Kindra Judd looked over at Marlo, who had just given her the best lovemaking session ever, and said, "I would love to become part of this family. If you guys will have me?"

Felita had heard what she thought she'd heard. And though surprised, for some reason, she wasn't as startled as someone living on the outside of the law should've been. In fact, she embraced the woman, so tightly, the knot holding Kindra's towel in place was un-lodged, falling to the carpet and exposing her.

"I guess that means I'm part of the family...?" Kindra Judd said, kneeling down without shame.

Felita said, "If that's what you told your peeps, I don't see why not..."

Chapter 24

SUNDAY MORNING @ 11:47
SIX WEEKS LATER ...

"In case your situ-ation has turned up-side-down, and all that you've accomplished is now-on-the-ground, you don't have to stay in the shape that you're in. Because, the Potter wants to put you back together again.

"Ooooh...the Potter waaaannnnts to put you back together aaggggain."

The sun sat in the beautiful blue sky over Jubilee Baptist Church. Everyone in the congregation was full of joy and spirit, as Rita and the choir sang the closing verses to the song, *The Potter's House*.

While they sang, Reverend Reeves got up and made his way to the alter. He was decked out in a navy blue suit tailor made by Ferragamo. The cocoa butter he applied to his skin had his head shining bright as the sun above. Man, was he sharp.

"Sing it, choir!" he shouted in his anointed reverend's tone, that no one but God could've given his as such a gift. Fulfilling the Reverend's request, Rita and the choir sang in harmony – "*The potter wants to put-you-back, to-gether-agaaain ... Ooooh ...the potter waaants to put-you- back- to gether aaagain.*"

As Doug orchestrated the choir with his hands, he

gave them the signal to get ready to close out. In their black and gold robes, Rita and the choir sat down in unity. Lawrence, Charles, and the rest of the musicians continued to keep the congregation swaying from side to side to the instrumental.

While the Reverend flipped through the Bible to bring a word from the Lord, his diamond rings sparkled on his hands. Once he came across the scripture that he was going to preach on, Reverend Reeves took a few seconds to observe his congregation. On the floor, he seen some crying as the music played, with their hands extended towards the heavens. In the mezzanine, some prayed while others looked at him as if he was the savior God sent to cater to their spiritual needs. The Reverend had a new perspective as far as what his church meant to him. Especially, after the conversation he had with Edward Haywood.

No way was he giving up his church for the dope game. Just that fast he learned something from a much younger man. And that was—practice what you preach. Straddling the fence wasn't what God had ordained him for. Deep down inside, Reverend Earl Reeves thanked Edward Haywood for a true reality check. Just looking over the congregation, the Reverend seen how blessed he was. So this sermon that he was about to preach was for the congregation, but mainly for himself.

Reverend Reeves looked back at Doug, which was also the signal to close out the music. Once Doug gave the order, the music ceased, and the Reverend adjusted the microphone to bring a message from the Lord.

"Good morning!!! Congregation!" Reverend Reeves roared. He was usually calm and humble, but not today.

"*Good morning*!" the congregation roared back. The 4,300 felt more like 43,000 this day.

"The potter wants ... to put you back together again," the Reverend stated clearly. 'How many of you know who *the potter* is?" He then added, "His name is Jesus. Come on, and say it with me!"

"*Jeeesus*!" the congregation shouted.

"Look at your life today, and compare it to the years gone by," the Reverend urged them, leaning into the microphone. "Ain't he good???"

"*Yesssss!*" almost everyone replied, dressed in their Sunday's best.

"I saaaaid, ... *ain't he good*???" the Reverend asked again. "Now what is his name???"

"His name is *Jesus*!" the congregation clarified.

"Amen...amen...*amen*," Reverend Reeves whispered deeply into the mic, as beads of sweat began to become visible on his shiny forehead. "Now, if you will...please turn your bibles to the book of Jerimiah, Chapter 18, verses 1-5."

He looked over the congregation as they flipped pages and hurried to find the scriptures. The Reverend even noticed Marlo, Nu-Nu, Felita, and Kindra with their heads buried in bibles. That made his smile.

"If you have it say, *Amen*!"

Once again, loudly, the congregation said, "*Amen*!"

The Reverend Reeves began to read -- "This is the word that came to Jeremiah from the Lord: *Go down to*

Potter's house, and there I will give you my message so I went down to the potter's house, and I saw him working at the wheel. But...the pot he was shaping from the clay was marred in his hands; so the potter formed it into another pot, shaping it as seemed best to him. Then the word of the Lord came to me. He said: "Can I not do with you, Isreal, as this potter does?" declared the Lord. "Like the clay in the potter's hand, so are you in my hand, Isreal." Then, Reverend Reeves said sternly, "You may close your bibles."

As he closed his bible along with the rest of the congregation, Reverend Reeves took a few more seconds to observe as many facial expressions as he could find. He looked at Rita and the choir, he checked out the musicians, and his Deacons, the missionaries and trustees, before finally giving his attention back to the members in the front row.

"What we have going on here in the *Old Testament*, in Jeremiah, which speaks of the potter...clay is being transformed into a vessel," the Reverend preached, as he looked back towards the pews. "When the potter receives this clay, it's a messy situation. But, it's something that the potter sees in the mess."

Queenie and Keith sat on the front row as Reverend Reeves put his sermon down. For some reason, Queenie noticed a different look in his eyes. The short and tight tan skirt she wore didn't attract his attention the way skirts not nearly as short had in the past. All she knew was he wasn't her Earl. He was the man God anointed to be a Reverend. She continued to watch him intently, and with her legs crossed tightly.

Right next to her, her brother, though still looking into his bible, held a deep scowl on his face. He wasn't reading scripture, nor was he listening to his Reverend. Keith was plotting his next move. There was no way he was going to be shown up and dismissed, without someone else at least feeling what he was feeling. He thought sending his sister that text, and convincing one of the Deacons to get the First Lady to the *sing off*, would have gotten the Reverend jammed up, both his women in the same place at the same time, thinking they were summoned to support him in a time of turmoil. But chess playing Earl was just a bit sharper that day. Keith wasn't done though. Nowhere close.

"So, he takes time to put this mess on his wheel," the Reverend continued to preach. "As the wheel is spinning, the potter puts his hands in this mess."

The congregation looked on, giving the Reverend their undivided attention. Not even a toddler could be heard weeping. It was so quiet, as he brought the message, that a stomach could be heard growling.

"As the potter is shaping and forming this clay with his hands..." He asked the faithful members as he looked around, "What is this clay saying?"

The congregation looked around at one another, as if they were lost. And certainly most were.

"The clay would say—oooch!!! Because...change hurts. And, in order for this mess to be shaped into something special, ...the potter has to slick his hand in and shape it," the Reverend shared, as he began to stalk towards the steps of the pulpit. "When we look at our lives, when we came to God, a lot of us was a mess."

Marlo and Kindra looked at one another as they sat and digested all that the Reverend was saying, while he made his way down the steps, now holding the microphone extra tight. For the first time, Officer Kindra Judd saw them as a sparkling family, *in their home.* Not some street hooligans destined for the penitentiary. And she did not regret compromising the investigation, as she knew that had she been looking more for the *not so good things*, instead of searching for the good, some-thing would have come up. But, *God works in myst-erious ways.*

"But, once we allow God to stick his hand in our lives, at times it may hurt, ... we may find ourselves on his wheel all alone. The blessing is -- *change has come.* Congregation, look at your neighbor, and say, *change is coming.*"

Each and every member followed his instructions, except Keith.

Reverend Reeves began to preach more, saying, "I remember ... back in the day ...when ... I was down and out in my life. I chose the wrong path ... which landed me in prison..."

As he got crunk, the whole congregation began to stand, shout, and raise their hands. Lawrence and the musicians began to play to his sermon.

"I came to the Lord in a mess," Reverend Reeves confessed, as he began to walk back and forth with ample purpose. "My emotions were cold. I was spiritually bankrupt. My relationship with Eva was on the rocks..."

Eva cried as she stood to her feet. She loved when her husband preached fire and brimstone, which was just the way God had intended. She knew he wasn't perfect by any stretch of the imagination, and that he had a multitude of shortcomings, but she would rather be with him when the potter was finished with him, than to not be.

"I was in a cell ... and I said ... Lord, I surrender ... my life is in a mess ... take me as I am ..."

All of the Reverend's staff shouted as they stood behind him in the pulpit.

"Once I surrendered – *huh*! God began to stick his hands in my mess – *huh*! He began to shape – *huh*! And mold me – *huh*! And look at me today –*huh*!"

People began to run up and down the aisles while others caught the holy spirit right where they stood. Not Keith. Queenie remained seated, with her head hanging low as the Reverend said, "No longer am I in bondage – *huh*! My emotions are in tack – *huh*! Today ... I'm spiritually rich ... and my relationship is now a beautiful marriage – *huh*! God couldn't have blessed me with such a special woman – *huh*!"

As she stood, Queenie looked over at Keith. Feeling convicted, she surrendered and began to respect the Reverend's marriage, due to his sermon. Suddenly, she grabbed her purse and headed up the aisle towards the doors of the church, leaving Keith behind.

Reverend Reeves was on fire, continuing with, "If...

you've been on drugs – *huh*! It's not too late – *huh*! If you have a drinking problem – *huh*! It's not too late – *huh*! If your bills outweigh your income – *huh*! It's not too late – *huh*!"

Nu-Nu cried as he stood and clapped his hands, while Felita jumped up and down full of the spirit. The little boy from Braggtown projects was seated with them, looking really nice in his new blue suit. Nu-Nu and Felita had taken the boy in. Turned out, the boy whose name was Le'Bron, named after the NBA superstar, was only 12 years old, and hadn't seen his parents in years. He now had a home, and a family to call his own.

"Let Him mold you – *huh!* Let Him shape you – *huh*! He cares – *huh*! God is the potter – *huh*! He wants you in his hands – *huh*! Say - *Je-suuuus*! *Je-suuuus*! *Amen*! *Amen*! *Aaaaaamen*!"

Once the Reverend closed out the sermon, the musicians began to crank up. To every tune and beat, people continued to dance and shout. It was one lady in a blue and black dress; she ran around the church shouting. Before Reverend Reeves could get up the steps to the pulpit, she ran and grabbed him. "*Thank you Lord*!" she yelled as she hugged the Reverend. "*Lord, I thank you for the word! My life is in a mess!!*"

The loud music, shouting, and clapping caused Reverend Reeves not to identify the lady's voice. He couldn't see her face either. Because it was covered by a Fendi net hat that shielded her features.

All of the Deacons came down and tried to pry the woman's hands from the Reverend's jacket sleeve.

"If you would just release the Reverend, we will not be forced to restrain you," a huge fellow in his most professional voice warned. And the woman complied. The Reverend was then escorted back up to the pulpit.

As he made his way to the Alter, Reverend Reeves straightened his suit out. Eva also stood at the Alter, so she could embrace her husband.

The congregation knew that Reverend Reeves was about to open the doors of the church. But, they weren't ready yet. It was as if they were rejoicing in heaven.

Speaking into the microphone, over all the rejoicing, Reverend Reeves said, before passing the mic to the First Lady, "Honey, take us out in prayer."

"Let us bow our heads," Eva began as Rita and the choir commenced to softly sing *The Potter's House*. "Father God, in the name of Jesus, whose love and blessings are far beyond measure. We thank you for the powerful sermon that you delivered through my husband. Lord, we know through all of our shortcomings, by you being the potter, there is no doubt that you can put us back together again. You're the alpha and the omega. Lord, you're the Beginning and the End. Our King of Kings. And, Lord of Lords. We thank you for your unspeakable joy and glory. In your namesake, we say—AMEN!"

Once Eva closed out the prayer, some people in the congregation began to embrace one another, while others talked and shook hands. That's when Gloria decided to pull her friend to the side.

"Eva, I have figured out why the offering was short, and for so long, without anyone taking notice," Gloria whispered into Eva's ear.

"Really?" Eva said, trying to keep an eye on Reverend Reeves. "And why is the offering short?"

"Well, it's simple math. Addition by subtraction. The woman in charge of the usher board—"

"Mrs. Marjorie? She just up and left town about two months ago," Eva recalled and told Gloria.

"When she left town, the offering went through the roof." Gloria was dressed in her Sunday's best, and looking Eva square in the eye. "She was helping herself to your husband's money."

"Oh," Eva sighed. *Earl really liked that woman too*, she was thinking as she covered her mouth.

"I guess my job is done here," Gloria said then hugged her friend. Gloria wanted to say more, but the look in Eva's eyes said end things there.

As people poured out of the church, Marlo and Nu-Nu left Kindra and Felita behind, and made their way through the crowd towards their uncle as he was walking down the steps of the pulpit, heading towards his chambers. Eva was trailing them, but decided to have a moment alone.

Seeing his nephews coming his way, Reverend Reeves nodded his head, signaling for them to follow him. Even with his nephews on his heels, the Reverend was still being mobbed by the crowd. Everyone wanted to talk and shake his hand.

Keith was leading the pack. "Reverend Reeves," he began, "is there by any chance you could speak with me? It is of extreme importance."

Reverend Reeve's eyes got wide as saucers. And his nephews took notice. He had to play it cool though, because it wasn't them he was worried about, it was the other members wanting to chat with him taking notice.

"Yes, Keith. I do have a few minutes for you."

They stepped to the side where no one could hear them, and Keith said, "Rita earned her spot. But I didn't deserve to be dismissed; not when I can destroy you within minutes."

"Are you threatening me?" Reverend Reeves whispered back, in a real cool tone.

"I'm just stating the facts. I think you should reconsider my position, and announce to the congregation next week, that I was only taking a break, and will be back from hiatus next month."

"Do you know Lawrence?"

"Do you know Queenie?"

Reverend Reeves sighed. He knew this day could come. And, he wasn't prepared. Have Lawrence make Keith disappear, because he couldn't keep his junk in his pants; or let Keith blackmail him and continue to put the church in turmoil???

The Reverend began to finger his goatee, just a staring down on Keith scrawny frame. "Lawrence is going to contact you. Give me a few days."

"Three days," Keith said, then pranced off smiling.

The Reverend went in the opposite direction, with Nu-Nu and Marlo tailing him. Once they made it to the chambers, Reverend Reeves said, "Close the door."

With the door shut tight, the Reverend said, "Take a seat." Both walked over and sat on the couch, full of curiosity, which was written all over their faces.

The Reverend stood with his back towards them, while he looked out his office window at the rejoiced people conversing, as they walked to their vehicles.

"Marlo, Nu-Nu, the game is over," he stated turning around to face them. "The well has run dry."

Marlo looked at Reverend Reeves with wrinkles across his forehead. "Unc, what are you talking about?"

"The connect is dead...so the came is over," he clarified, walking towards them. "We all made plenty money. Now it's time to live righteous."

"What are you saying?" Nu-Nu demanded to know.

"God works in mysterious ways," Reverend Reeves said, taking a seat in his leather recliner. "He's done for me what I couldn't do for myself. So, I'm out."

Marlo and Nu-Nu looked at one another, as visions of their reign coming to an end hit them like a ton of bricks. They loved and respected their uncle, but they also loved and respected the game. There were people who depended on them to eat. But, they put up no resistance as their heads dropped in defeat. And almost at the same time, they both wondered *had Felita told the Reverend that Kindra Judd was a cop*, after they had all agreed the Reverend didn't need to know that just yet—if ever.

Crossing his leg, one over the other, as if he was Don Corleone, Reverend Reeves said, “I’m giving you two the condo. A gift from me and your aunt.”

The condominium had been part of the Reverend and Eva’s portfolio for several years. It’s where they began their journey of home owning. It held many memories and sentimental value. It was worth a quarter mil’ easy. But, the Reverend knew it would be in good hands, and they would appreciate it. Plus, if the boys ever went into financial turmoil, they could sell it. They’d helped the Reverend and Edwards make millions.

Both of his nephews were unable to contain their happiness, and bum-rushed the Reverend, nearly knocking him out his chair.

They helped him up, and he said, “That’s not it.” The Reverend went to a painting of Jesus and lifted it from the wall. Behind it was a safe. While the Reverend pressed buttons on the keypad, again Marlo and Nu-Nu looked at one another.

Once the safe was open, Reverend Reeves pulled out ten stacks of banned up money. He closed the safe, put the painting back, and walked over to his nephews.

“This is a hundred thousand. Let start a business. A family business, that you and those beautiful women, and the boy, can benefit from. Maybe a restaurant, or arcade or something nice like that.”

“My niggah!” Marlo rejoiced.

“Yessss!” Nu-Nu interjected.

Both of them had some money put up, but opening

a business would have financially crippled them if the business didn't flourish. This was better than being in the drug game, and they wished their uncle had done it sooner.

As soon as his nephews left, Eva appeared with a long face. She said, "I'm going to the nursery home with a few missionaries. We're going to pass out some goody bags, and share the word. I'll be home right after that. We need to talk."

The Reverend hoped Keith hadn't forced his hand, by reneging on their little agreement. He hadn't seen Eva look so sad in many years. He pulled her in from the doorsill, and shut the door. "I love you more than anything in this world. And I would never do anything to intentionally hurt you."

Eva smiled, said, "You're gonna be the one hurt. Because I know you trusted this woman. And sometimes we think we know people, but we really don't. "

Before the Reverend could say anything, she ended with, "I'll see you when I get home. They're waiting on me."

As the Reverend's head dropped, as if he didn't already have enough on his plate, Eva doubled back and said, "Oh, there's a new member I think you would like to talk to."

The Reverend was always looking forward to meeting new members. That meant not only would his percentage go up towards the offering, but he could possibly change someone's life as well. But this day, he wasn't in the mood. Yet, he said, "Please, send them in. Would you please?" he replied, while containing the fire roaring within.

In a flash, Eva was back with the new member. When Reverend Reeves saw that it was Sack, he kissed his wife's cheek, and said, "I'll see you later."

As soon as he shut the door behind the First Lady, he turned to Sack, and said, "If this is about Pokey, and nothing else, I suggest you leave now."

"This is about me and you, Earl. By the way, nice, nice sermon. I must say so myself."

The Reverend almost said, *bullshit*, but continued to contain the flames burning inside him. He knew the Lord was testing him. "What about me and *you*, Sack?"

"I take that sharp nephew of yours never gave you my message." After Sack said that, he went behind the Reverend's desk, and sat in his chair. *Talk about disrespect.* Then Sack said, "I bought this suit with some of the hush money your nephew gave me."

The Reverend was fuming now. "Hush money?"

"Yeah. I had enough to get me this suit, a few rocks, pay Laverne for giving me some of them guts. You do know *Laverne*, don't you? Of course you do—you tried to get you some of them guts, according to her."

"Sack if you don't get out my seat, talking that nonsense, I'm gonna be forced to remove by force."

"All I want is some help, brother. You helped everyone else—"

Reverend Reeves marched around the huge desk, and

snatched Sack by the lapels of his cheap suit, and lifted him from the chair. “If you are not here with good intentions, especially with the mood I am in, I suggest you leave.”

Sack lifted his hands to the Lord, and said, “Does that mean, you are refusing to help me?”

“Help you with what?” the Reverend asked, releasing Sack’s blazer.

“You hooked Pokey up with Eva’s sister, when it should’ve been me. You took him to Disney World, when it should’ve been me. You got him moving the best coke in town—“

“Sack, I am asking you to leave for the last time.”

“At least tell me you believe me, that Pokey was trying to send you back up to Bunn. I am not making this up,” Sack said, looking the Reverend straight in the eyes. “I am not here to hurt you—“

“So this isn’t a half baked shakedown?”

“No, I actually hoped you would help me out,” Sack stated unconvincingly.

Reverend Reeves pulled this fat wallet from his back pocket, and took all the money from it, and said, “I hope this will help you.” It was about $2,000. If Sack turned it down, the Reverend planned on helping him. But it Sack took it, then it would be the last time they even speak.

“Thank you, Earl,” Sack said, fingering the mitt as he grinned taking baby steps towards the door.

With not much force, the Reverend grabbed Sack by the arm. He patted Sack down, checked him for a wire, then said, "I never wanna see you again."

"You didn't want to see me in the first place. I just got lucky, being in the right place at the right time," Sack said, with a scowl. "All Earl cares about is Earl. Everybody knows that, but you. Goodbye, Earl."

And just like that, Sack was gone as fast as he had come. Just as the Reverend was about to sit down and sulk in his sudden misery, another knock came at the door. He started to ignore it, but he remembered Eva said new members. More than one. He opened the door and in waltzed, Pokey.

"Pokey!" the Reverend exclaimed.

Eva was in the background, and could not contain her smile. She slowly pulled the door back shut, and headed to the nursing home to her charitable deed.

Pokey was dressed in a nice brown suit with black dress shoes. He was nice and clean shaven. His complexion was now clear. Seeing him clean, brought tears to the Reverend's eyes. He ran over and hugged his best friend. Although he knew Pokey was in rehab for six weeks, Reverend Reeves still patted Pokey down. Simple and plain, he was paranoid.

Pokey said, "LeBron led Nu-Nu to me, and when I saw him I was in tears…"

At the very same time, Nu-Nu had got a call from Felita informing him about what she had heard the girl in the bathroom tell Marlo. It was the best thing that could have happened for Pokey.

"God, thank you," Reverend Reeves stated, and then quoted the scripture Luke 15, Verse 4-7 into Pokey's ear. "*Suppose one of you has a hundred sheep and loses one of them. Doesn't he leave the ninety-nine in the open country and go after the lost sheep until he finds it, he joyfully puts it on his shoulders and goes home. Then he calls his friends and neighbors together and says – Rejoice with me; I have found my lost sheep. I tell you that in the same way there will be more rejoicing in heaven over one sinner who repents than over ninety-nine righteous persons who do not need to repent.*"

Then Reverend Reeves added, "Welcome to the flock, Pokey. Welcome back to the flock."

"I love you, Earl. And I would never cross you. But I was weak. And now I am strong."

"I know, Pokey," the Reverend whispered, praying that Pokey's words were true.

Pokey told him who the cop was and what he wanted him to do. Explained that he kept the buy money, so there could be no *buy and bust*. And almost in an instant, worry no longer roamed the Reverend's brain cells. But he did acknowledge that Sack was willing to see Pokey in a ditch just so he could come up; and that it was never about protecting the Reverend's interests.

Not only did he began to change for the future chapters in his life, Reverend Reeves was going to do all that he could to bring more colorful chapters to Pokey's life, instead of using him for his personal gain. *Basically paying him below wages, and with drugs.*

As he closed the door to leave his chambers, the Reverend could hear loud cries along with chatter. He made his way back towards the sanctuary. Once he entered, he noticed that Edward, Rita and Lawrence were talking to a man and a woman. Reverend Reeves couldn't identify who they were because their backs were turned to him. All the Reverend knew was, that while Rita was crying and hugging Edward, Lawrence had his hands raised up thanking God.

"What is going on?" Reverend Reeves asked, in suspense, as he quickly strutted towards them.

Once he got up on the man and the woman, he noticed who they were. While Rita continued to cry and hug Edward in a tight embrace, the Reverend stood in awe. He could not believe what he was witnessing.

David and Tamela Mann!

Not only did they do gospel inspirational plays, they also starred in a lot of Tyler Perry's movies. Tamela Mann also was one of Kirk Franklin's star singers. Her biggest hit was *Take Me to the King*. In two month time, the song went platinum.

By Edward once having a studio, not only did he have connections with producers in New York, he also had contacts with LA Reid in Atlanta. After telling LA Reid about the sing off, and how Rita blew the roof off, the music exec contacted David and Tamela Mann. They couldn't rest until they heard Rita's voice. The way that Rita sang for them without music, all David and Tamela could do was sign her to a contract.

In shock, Reverend Reeves inquired, "What brings such huge stars to Jubilee Baptist? I'm Reverend Earl Reeves." He then extended his hand for a shake.

"Good afternoon, Reverend Reeves. That was a beautiful sermon you delivered," David replied, as his wife looked on with a wide smile. "We heard a lot about this young lady, through brother Edward, and we decided to sign her to a record deal."

Tamela continued to smile and nod her head. It was as if she was the fan and Rita was the star.

Releasing her embrace with Edward, Rita ran over and hugged the Reverend while raining tears on his suit. Reverend Reeves didn't want to lose Rita. But he knew that this was a blessing from God. After all that she been through—emotional abuse, the cheating, being let go from her job, struggling with weight—she deserved it. Rita had overcome the odds.

The Reverend knew that his counseling played a major part in her not giving up on herself and turning to drugs. He wanted to be selfish, keep her to himself. But that wouldn't have been of God though. All he could do was thank God that he could be part of something so beautiful. *It also gave him an out with Keith.*

Only something of that magnitude could take the Reverend's mind away from Keith's threats of exposition, Sack's blackmail attempt, and Pokey's lapse of judgment. Softly, the Reverend whispered into Rita's ear, "Stop crying, you deserve this. You deserve it."

"If it wasn't for you, Rev," she wept, continuing to cling to him, "I'd be all messed up..."

Edward and Lawrence stood and watched, as Reverend Reeves and Rita embraced, and noticed the tears falling from the Reverend's eyes.

The Reverend was human. In order to not let his flesh get in get in the way, he released his embrace slowly, and kissed Rita on the cheek. He noticed that she had lost about forty pounds too, and smiled.

Turning around, he shook David and Tamela's hand. Afterwards, he shook Edward and Lawrence's hand. The Reverend then made his way up the aisle and headed towards the doors of the church, as he heard David began to talk to Rita.

Once he got outside the church and strolled towards his Navigator, the Reverend stared in surprise. *Queenie must be pissed*, he reasoned, noticing that she left the shoes he'd purchased her on the hood of his truck. There was also a letter up under the driver's side windshield wiper. The Reverend was glad that Eva or any other member of the congregation peeped what was going on. He would've been evicted from his home, and the church. He took one last look to make sure no one was looking.

Someone was…

Officer Jamie Green was holding a pair of binoculars and watching Reverend Reeves intently. He just wasn't buying Kindra Judd's reporting that she was unable to corroborate Pokey's original statement. And after finding out that she was still seeing the Marlo dude, having turned her report in, he continued to investigate.

Quickly, Reverend Reeves walked over to his vehicle, hit the alarm, and the door switch on his key. The Reverend grabbed the three boxes of pumps, opened the door, and tossed them on the passenger seat.

Glaring around this time, the Reverend snatched the letter from the windshield and began to read.

Earl,

the love of my life. Hearing the sincerity in your sermon today caused me to also see the sincerity in your eyes. All you preached came from your big heart. I don't know if you noticed or not, but I felt bad and left church early. Feeling convicted, all I could do was sit and cry in my car. You spoke of the potter. Can he replace this void in my life? Earl, I do love you. I'm accepting the fact that I'm the mess on the potter's wheel. Chance is going to hurt. Thanks for making me feel so special. Congrats…I thought it would've been me.

Love , Queenie

"Daaammn," the Reverend said quietly, as he balled the letter up in his palm. Staring off into space, it was as if he couldn't move. He was still loving Queenie, and did not anticipate her breaking things off. For him, this was a devastating loss. Three years of sneaking around had turned to love. Finally, he tried to board his vehicle, still holding onto the ball of paper. Normally he broke things off, and not the other way around.

"*Earl,*" he heard a familiar voice chime from behind him. "*This is my tithe for the church…*"

Turning around, the Reverend noticed that it was the woman in the blue dress with the Fendi net hat. All he could do was smile and stare, to shield the pain Queenie had left him with. "Ma'am, all of my ushers are gone. Either you can put it in next Sunday, or you can just give it to me."

The woman then dug deep down in her purse and stated in an angry tone, "That's damn sure what I'm going to do. This tithe is just for you…"

Seeing the woman whip out a pearl handled .25 automatic, and raise the net of the hat from her face, Reverend Reeves almost pissed in his pants. He saw that the woman was Marjorie. She now had the pistol aimed directly at his chest. "Now, I've got a sermon for your ass, ole Earl, or should I say *Reverend Reeves*?"

"Marjorie...Marjorie...wh-what is going on?" he quizzed, in a state of panic. His heart rate began to soar.

"You tell me," she spat back defiantly. "I guess your ass is about to go on to hell with my husband – *huh*?" Before he could say a word, Marjorie added as she braced her arm and gripped the pistol tighter, "Why do men...play with my feelings, Earl???"

Reverend Reeves began to plead, "Look, Marjorie, whatever I've done to you, I sincerely apologize."

"Apologies my ass," she stated coldly, with the pistol trained on the Reverend. "You wasn't apologetic when you had unprotected sex with me, were you Earl???"

Reverend Reeves was convicted. His sins had finally caught up to him, and were slapping him in the face. Seeing the crazed look in Marjorie's eyes, he felt it was best he just kept his mouth shut.

Marjorie shouted, "*Earl*...do you hear me talking to you? *Huhhhh*???"

The Reverend felt a calm and holy spirit come over him. Slowly, he closed his eyes and said a prayer of repentance. If that was the day to meet the maker, he wanted to be on the right side of God.

Officer Jamie Green couldn't believe his eyes. His leg began to fidget, his foot began to bounce rapidly. He remembered visiting Marjorie's home some time back about her husband's violent death. Officer Green called for backup and darted from his car just as he witnessed

Marjorie pull the trigger. All the Reverend heard was: *POOOOW!*

Opening his eyes, he saw that Marjorie had shot herself in the face. Hearing the loud sound, Edward and Lawrence darted from the church. Rita, David, and Tamela were on their heels, moving fast as well.

"Someone please call 911!" Reverend Reeves shouted in disbelief while standing over her. "Mrs. Marjorie has shot herself!"

As Rita obliged the Reverend, she pushed David and Tamela back inside the church. Edward and Lawrence slowly made their way over to the scene. "Earl … what happened?" Lawrence asked while Edward stood beside him. Both men were puzzled, but there to aid the Reverend in any way possible.

Officer Green was out of breath by the time he reached the crime scene. He was brandishing his weapon and his shield, damn near leaning over.

The Reverend was saying, "All I know is she was confessing her sins, and then she killed herself." He pretended to weep a bit, then told Edward, "Let's get ready to have a service for one of God's anointed."

"Back UP! Help is on the way!" Officer Green shouted exuding his authority. He then kicked the gun from Marjorie's side where it had fallen. "This is a crime scene!"

The three men stood and mourned together, over Mrs. Marjorie's body. Reverend Reeves was sad, but he was also glad that their secret was now going to the grave. From that day forward, he planned to walk in the light as a Reverend should.

And then Green checked her vitals. "She still alive!" he alarmed everyone in earshot. Next, he administered CPR. Sirens could be heard shrilling in the distance before the red, white and blue lights began to bounce off everything in the vicinity.

An EMT truck, several cop cruisers, followed by a fire truck, pulled up. Officer Green gave them the rundown as Marjorie was being strapped to a gurney. She was swooped up and loaded onto the EMT truck as the Reverend stood not far away with his mouth agape.

"She's breathing," the Reverend heard a young Asian EMT worker announce. "She's going to make it."

Green slapped on some latex gloves and retrieved the gun, not waiting for the crime scene unit to arrive. He turned to Reverend Reeves and said, "I'm gonna need a statement from you, *mister*."

"I didn't see anything. My eyes were shut, *mister*," the Reverend quickly replied back.

Officer Green said, "Well, did you hear anything? Did she say anything?"

Wasting no time, the Reverend said, "Nothing…"

The Epilogue

THREE MONTHS LATER…

Turned out, the gun Marjorie had shot herself with was the very same gun used in her husband's homicide.

Marjorie was charged with murder, and reached out to the church for support. She threatened the Reverend with exposing him if he didn't provide character testimony on her behalf.

Reverend Reeves thought he had been freed of Marjorie's madness. Yes, he was fornicating with a mad woman. He couldn't believe she had killed her husband, *and* kept the gun.

Reverend Reeves was preparing to supply statements from Ushers, Deacons, the First Lady and himself, when he was informed that Marjorie had been stealing from the church for years. He felt like a fool. *She was spending my money on me!*, he had sulked over some cookies and milk one night.

Although Officer Green didn't get the result he desired with Pokey, he had been promoted for making the arrest in the unsolved murder of Marjorie's husband. The first person he called was Kindra Judd, who was battling morning sickness. *Yes*, she and Marlo were expecting their first child together.

"I owe you, Officer Judd," *now* Detective Green had told Kindra. "*See you soon…*" Whatever that was supposed to mean.

Kindra Judd admired Felita's toughness, and the street smarts she mixed with her spirituality, and asked Felita to be the godmother. Felita was elated. And so was Nu-Nu.

At the same time, Rita was asking Edward to become her manager. She had lost so much weight, Rita was getting request to do print modeling for high fashion designers.

Edward and Reverend Earl Reeves went on to save many lives, while Marjorie received 20 years in prison. She eventually pled out after the Reverend dared her to speak about his sins. She knew she would have to mention her thievery, if she had.

But…just when Marjorie was convinced that she was all alone, she got a surprise visit from Keith. *Being reassigned to lead the choir wasn't going to fix the pain Reverend Reeves caused his family.*

From the heart,

First and foremost, I must and will give God the glory and credit. It's such a blessing to be part of S.G. Publishing. Collaborating with BOOG DENIRO was a dream of a lifetime. Thank you Lord for giving me the gifts of ambition, literacy, and vivid imagination. Because of you Father God, me and BOOG brought The Ungodly Pastor from vision to reality. Now. I want to travel by deep gratitude. From 95 North down to 85 South. All I say comes from love the utmost respect. Instead of tearing me down, these people built me up.

Omar Jennett & Naquan Crocker, thanks for welcoming me into your heart and lives. I consider you family. Forever loyalty is deeply rooted in my soul for S.G. Publishing.

A special shout out to people I've worked with: Ms. Tonya Ridley, Victor L. Martin, Marquis McKenzie, and Melvin Alston. Tonya, thank you for the love and support during my incarceration. While you were writing *Money Maker* you still took time out your busy schedule to read and coach me. You told me *if writing is my passion, don't stop.*

Victor, Marquis and Melvin, I'll never forget how we worked together constantly around the clock at Johnson County Correctional. Such a beautiful experience.

My beautiful grandmother, Mrs. Doris V. McRae, thanks for nurturing me with the very best love and support, that a grandson could ever imagine. Also, know as well as anyone how long I've been in pursuit of this dream.

Got to thank my aunt Sandra McRae for always believing in me. Your motivation inspires me to all that I can be.

To all my aunts and uncles, love you! No longer around, but still he watches over me, uncle John Allen McRae. Rest in peace.

Gotta give my cousin Lamont McRae his props. The best cousin God could give a person. My other cousins, nieces, nephews, we from the south. Too many to name.

Never will I forget the Kerrwood crew: Stephen James, Kamal, Gerald, Calio, Josh Cotton, Dee Lynn, Denard Niko, Boot Devine, Ms. Blondine Pollard, Ms. Carolyn Judd, Keisha Judd (RIP), Ms. Alice Whitaker, Ms. Emma Devine, Ms. Wendy Adams, Cliff and Chuck Manning, AB, D-Wall, Coon Dog. My well known circle.

Big shouts to Lex, Face, Maintain, Utz, Meech, Philly Black, Wise, Melvin, Styles, Ice, Pac, Gator, Troy, Gibby, Butch, Boney, Shaq, NY Black, Raw, Chitown G. All of you guys took me into your hearts and helped me through my struggles.

Last but not least, thanx to Ms. Nancy Byrd and Fam. Always through the storms of life you stuck by me no matter what. A blessing to me. Love is the shackle that keeps us together forever.

I also want to send a shout out to Mr. and Mrs. Ed and Jan Efurd of Dothan, Alabama. Thanks for hanging with me through it all. And to Ben Efurd you'll always be my brother from another mother.

If it's anyone I didn't mention, please don't take it personal. I'm just excited!

Country McRae

Boog Deniro's thoughts...

It was truly a joy to work on ***The Ungodly Pastor***. The development of the characters, the plot, the message, the editing, the typesetting—all of it!!! The final product is superlative entertainment, that I am extremely proud of. Thank you, Country McRae. This was your idea, Unk! We got 4 more project to go!!!

Shout outs to—my partner Omar, my beloved sister Naquan, the legendary DJ Cocoa Chanelle, my attorney Roy Galloway, my bro Robert Wiesman, DJ Waffles, Rah the Boss (Left 4 Dead Films), Basilla, Nicole, Claudia, Ny Way, Takia, Dwayne Watkins, Shannon Holmes, Wahida Clark, Tisha, my guy Tankhead Genile, and Shalamar.

Now...an exclusive Sneak Peek of my next solo novel...

Infinite Addiction

A Romance for the Streets

CHAPTER ONE

"Imagine being locked away for seventeen-plus years for a crime you didn't commit, and sentenced to LIFE. While you're locked away, your foster mother succumbs to cancer, your father vanished without a trace. But somehow you manage to survive, and live as if you're freedom and dignity hasn't been stolen from you…

"After all, the criminal justice system is supposed to be about being fair and just…

"In this episode of *The Gorgeous Gangstas Podcast*, we bring you—Amar Durant. Amar was recently vindicated, and released from Somerset prison in the home state of Meek Mill," Miracle opened up with.

"Thank you, *ladies*, for having me," Amar said as he sat up, speaking directly into the bedazzled mic. It was a May evening, and Amar was dressed in all white, Gucci everything. May 31st, to be exact.

"*The Gorgeous Gangstas Podcast* is not a wrongful conviction platform. We give a platform to ex-cons who make positive contributions to our culture upon their release. Specifically men, and how they survived on the inside is important too.

"So, Amar …tell the listeners and the viewers, a little about yourself," Miracle further stated. Miracle had one of those soft and inviting voices.

Amar exhaled, smiling so wide, his pearly whites were visible for all to see. "Wow, where do we start?"

The Gorgeous Gangstas Podcast consisted of three women from the New York City area. One in her twenties, one in her thirties, and one in her forties. They had a very intimate set in a spacious Manhattan apartment, overlooking the Hudson River, a camera guy supplying visual support, episodes airing twice a week for nearly 200,000 listeners and viewers.

Miracle, who was 41, put you in the mind of Kandi of *Xscape* fame, and more recently *Atlanta Housewives*. Very vibrant, extremely attractive, super luscious, and so outspoken about her take on intimacy, best described Miracle.

Her co-host, and daughter, Dynasty, was 25, and a dead-ringer for KeKe Palmer's character in the hit Fox show *Star*. Dynasty had actually auditioned for a role on *Star* back in 2017. She was a go-getter, and a millennial to the heart.

The third co-host, Yolanda, should've been in Hollywood doing movies. But she loved the New York metropolis, where she learned the Radio Broadcasting business right before the boom of social media. Yolanda wore her blond mane in lengthy and lustrous curls, and was very much into her physical fitness. This 32-year old's figure was very, very lissome, with curve in all the right places. Yolanda was often referred to as …*White*

Chocolate by friends in the industry, because although she was a white girl, she had so much soul. Outside of *The Gorgeous Gangstas Podcast*, she also ran a successful publishing imprint that cranked out some of the steamiest erotica on the web, and bookshelves across the country.

Life was good for all three women. But doing the Podcast was what truly made these women happy.

All three women – Miracle, Dynasty, and Yolanda – concurred that a Gorgeous Gangsta is a male or female who has overcome some dire circumstances, attractive, and always kept it real no matter what. He or she had to be living a positive lifestyle, and also be using his or her platform in a positive way. Of the three seasons of *The Gorgeous Gangsta Podcast*, only one had featured female gangstas. Not because there weren't many women doing their thing, and survived some sort of calamity, persevering triumphantly. *That's gangsta*, no matter what gender you are. They just enjoyed telling the stories of gorgeous men. Once in a while, things would go further. But, they were always professional, and always thinking *career first*.

They had never affiliated with, associated with, or hosted a man who promoted violence or any kind of negativity. That's why their audience and platform was constantly growing, and well received by women of all ages and cultures.

Yolanda told Amar, "Start with your current status? Are you single, or bagged and tagged? That's what the ladies want to know since you coming home looking like a fresh gallon of milk."

"I am single," Amar revealed, reluctantly. He still couldn't get his ex-lover out his mind even though he'd been free for several months now, and had been seduced a few times.

Dynasty asked, "Why? You are a gorgeous man. And, you just worked on one of the hottest films to be shown at the *Sundance Film Festival.* I would think woman would be clamoring over you, Mr. Amar?"

Amar said, "Thank you." Then there was a pause before he added, "Right before I was vindicated, the young lady I was into left me. And I was deeply saddened by it."

"Really? I am sorry to hear that. Did she give you a reason why?" asked Miracle.

"Another brother. She said, *I love you*, but *you're there, he's here*," it pained Amar to state. "I was totally blindsided."

There was a quietness that took hold of the large room, and the camera man took that time to get a close up of Amar, and then the facial expressions of all three woman. Clearly, this was a moment of emotion the hosts, nor the guest, saw coming, even though Amar had the questions a week in advance.

"I spent five years of my life with a woman, whom I

truly adored, "Amar finally stated, regaining his poised posture and leveled delivery. "She wasn't super bad, or unrealistically high maintenance like la lot of women these days. But, she owned an attractiveness that could be appreciated."

"*Ooooh*," all three women said in unison.

Amar continued, articulately stating, "She was ten years younger than me. She wasn't petite, or *slim thick*, and had probably seen her better days as a *baddie* pass her by. But, I adored her for who she was."

"And of course, you met her while imprisoned?" Miracle asked, making sure the audience understood that dynamic of the relationship.

"*That is correct*."

Miracle said, "What were your thoughts when you first saw this woman in person? Not selfies?"

"It was obvious she had children. Her love handles were visible, and her stomach protruded a little. But I saw something else," Amar said swiftly.

"And what was that, Amar?" Dynasty leaned closer to her mic and asked, anticipating the response.

"That, she needed to be reminded that, although she wasn't fabulous by this new unrealistic social media standard, she was still adorable." Amar's voice and delivery was even-keeled and so honest.

"*Wow!*" the women said in unison again.

Unsolicited, and before the women could catch their breath, Amar added, "I saw a potential partner. A best friend. Not eye candy, or arm candy, or a chick cats seduce, exploit, then pass over. But, wholesome candy, the kind a mother would find tasteful when a brother introduces her to momz. I saw a woman I wanted to do everything with, and wouldn't mind doing anything for.

That is what I saw. Word up."

"Explain why?" Yolanda urged.

"Because I believed in my instinct, and my instinct said, *this woman would appreciate kindness.* My instinct said, *gifts will enrich her spirit, not inflate her ego.* And for the most part, I was right."

"*Really*," Yolanda said with a smirk and stirring in her swivel chair. "Do all men in prison seeking companionship speak so eloquently about women?"

Dynasty interjected with, "If they did, more women would probably be finding love *behind the wall.*"

Miracle was smiling too, and said, "Well, how did you meet this special woman you came to love so deeply?"

"Before finally meeting face to face, we spoke on the phone for a couple months. In the early morning, and all times into the night. We texted, we played phone tag, we even sent selfies," Amar explained while memories from those times momentarily played in his mind.

"That sounds more like a romance unfolding in the streets than it does a romance forming between a prisoner and a woman in the streets," Miracle opined, with her finger interlaced and under her chin. "No wonder you fell in love."

"Momma, let the man speak," begged Dynasty.

"Let me just say, it was special. At least, to me it was," Amar elaborated, looking in Dynasty's direction. All the women were attractive to Amar. But Dynasty was gorgeous. She was wearing a white cat-suit, had her hair in a sleek and low ponytail that showcased her facial features perfectly.

"So, you finally meet, what, on a visit, and what?" Miracle asked, smiling in her daughter's direction. She peeped Amar checking out her only offspring.

"I imagined her coming in some stilettoes, maybe a nice jean and top. But she appeared in some *Truck Fit* leggings and a *Truck Fit* Tee. Some low cut white ones. Hair and nails were done."

"What did you think?" Dynasty asked.

"She's down to earth. Relatable. Exactly who she told me she was. A woman still figuring things out. A woman raising her kids on her own. A woman unwilling to sugarcoat things, was candid about the insufficiencies in her life. And she took to my ability to really care."

"After the first date, I mean, first visit?" Miracle asked. This was by far the most vulnerable dialogue from a man who had spent time in prison. And many had come before Amar. She enjoyed tapping into the psyche of women who date men in prison, but nowhere near as much as why men fell for the women with blind faith.

Amar said, "Actually, I felt connected to her before the visit. That's why I was able to look pass any flaws."

"Could it be, you only looked pass the flaws because you were desperate?" Miracle questioned, then took a sip from her wine glass. The ladies had been sipping a fancy bottle of Moscoto.

"Actually, I was seeing several women when I met her," Amar made clear, but in a respectful way, not arrogantly. "And they were all attractive and had careers. My social media was popping. I had already secured deals for two of my screenplays. No, I was not desperate."

"Yeah, momma, look at this man. How could he be desperate? He had a cell phone in his cell. *Allegedly*."

"I second that," Yolanda chimed in.

Miracle had to make it interesting, to boost the ratings, to challenge perspectives, so she said, "He had a life sentence too. He could've been desperate, Dynasty. And, Yolanda."

"The only thing I was desperate for was my freedom," Amar proudly inserted into the mix. He knew Yolanda would take tough stances. He'd viewed some of their earlier work, to prepare himself. And it was the truth, he was only desperate for liberation. "When I met shorty, I was on the cusp of being freed. I just didn't know it would take five years. Like the brother Tysheem Crocker wrote, in his *Reasonable Diligence* book—*injustice is swift and deliberate, while justice is slow*. Shout out to all my guys up at SCI Somerset!"

"I really, really like the way this brother expresses himself," Yolanda admitted, then added, "I'm sure the mystery woman did too. So, the viewer would like to know, have you contacted her since your release?"

RESPECT THE STRUGGLE is fictional and unapologetically raw. A gripping tale of harsh realities and memorable characters coming of age. Set in the 90's, the protagonist is Tyreen "Ta-Ta" Carver, a Bronx, New York teen. He's telling this story sometimes in retrospect, and other times in the moment. It's about survival and persevering in a city where no one cares how you survived, only how you prospered.

At points, you'll experience laughter, or get teary eyed, remembering something similar happening to you. Overall, a very solid attmept at depicting the darker side of street life. *The struggle isn't just a place, it's where you earn your respect.*

STREET GENERALS ... Capri and Zest Haywood, first and only cousins, in their early twenties, are living the type of lifestyle fake thugs fantasize about, platinum selling rappers spit in their rhymes, and many lose liberty and life trying to attain. But swagger for days doesn't curb the appetite of guys like these. While the suspense will have you unable to sit the book down, the twists and turns will have readers trying to be psychic. These characters are so complex and seemingly real that the thin line between reality and fiction has been brilliantly blurred. Harlem, New York hadn't been hotter since the early 80's.

STREET GENERALS 2, Nothing Is Sacred! Nothing is sacred in Harlem. Not right now. Not with the Feds knowing so much, and coming on so strong. Not with prices on heads.

When Capri's girlfriend goes missing, the pretty gangsta finally realizes he may've bit off more than his jaws can handle. Things go from feeling like the entire universe is conspiring to help him conquer the gargantuan of Harlem's underworld, to feeling like the sky is falling atop his hard head. *The suspense is so elevated, the twists never stop, nights are sultry, tomorrow is an afterthought, and resolve just may never come.* Witness unparalleled street mettle!

Can't Stop Won't Stop, STREET GENERALS 3... Iris Mena moves up in the ranks of her male dominated crew, while at the same time trying to figure out her sexuality. With conservative parents, she also wrangles with other life choices.

The Street Generals crew are on course to even one last score, and then she's out. But, the unthinkable transpires. Between the car bombing, and an Amber Alert, a Special Crimes Unit hops on their trail.

Will Stink's sudden philanthropy and desire to save his marriage come a little too late?

And what about Capri? Has his growth finally been stunted?

Don't even try to predict this one!!!

BOOG DENIRO PRESENTS...

ANY DAY
CAN BE YOUR LAST
IN THE
JUNGLE

BY: DONTAY "3" DESHIELDS

S.G. PUBLISHING
BRONX NEW YORK

BOOG DENIRO PRESENTS ...

When the lions have conquered

every other animal in the jungle,

they feed on each other.

PROLOGUE

York, County
April 3, 2012 – 11:30 PM

The air was dry, the cocaine was potent, the walls were sweating, and Jewloni was getting more agitated as the seconds passed. He loved the money; Oh did he ever. However, the tedious task of putting everything in order was the worse part of his occupation.

He used the left sleeve of his shirt to wipe the sweat from his forehead, before compressing, stamping and packaging another, however, after recently being let go by the Atlanta Falcons, trapping paid the bills and kept a hold on the lavish lifestyle he had become accustom to.

Jewloni's iPhone chirped indicating that an incoming text message had arrived. Jewloni removed the latex gloves from his fingers and dried his sweaty palms off with his shirt.

The message was clear and direct, and from the bulge forming in his jeans, obviously he liked what he read.

It was on. Jewloni stopped what he was doing and rushed to go take a shower. He was going to take her up on the offer. Twenty minutes later, he was fully dressed and headed out the door. He climbed into his SUV and mashed the accelerator.

Route 30 was the stretch of highway he used regularly to get back and forth to the city. And it was during these 20 minute drives that he did his best gauging and preparation. But during this particular ride it wasn't business on his mind, it was pleasure. Not the kind that is usually equated with lust, but real chemistry. And he believed wholeheartedly that he was finally found that with Ashley.

She had been helping Jewloni mend the pieces of his life back together ever since his fall from stardom. She'd also been blessing him with toe curling head that had him open like 7/11. Ashley was quite aware of her effects on Jewloni. He knew it too, but he didn't care much. He was happy just as long as she kept giving him her incredible lips.

Jewloni couldn't find available parking so he cruised further up the street until he found one. It wasn't too far from the club where Ashley insisted they meet. He actually loved the nightlife, so he didn't protest. Instead he put on his best, then lined his pockets with big faces, anticipating another ball out night.

When he finally reached the club, he noticed an older crowd and that the atmosphere was a lot more laxed. The bar was crowded, females dancing and everyone enjoying themselves. He searched the sea of fine sisters but couldn't find Ashley anywhere so he took the first empty booth. Ten minutes became twenty, and then an hour had passed. Jewloni decided to leave, unable to accept the fact that Ashley had stood him up. He couldn't wait to see her so he could tell her about herself.

ONE
The Come Up

April 4, 2102 – 12:32

The sound of thunder and flash of flames were the last thing many of Ahmad's victims saw and heard before meeting their maker. This evening would be no different. Ahmad pulled his 70's model Gran Torino to the curb and toked on some haze while waiting for his victim to show face.

From the intel, Gus', a local hot spot on the westside of York was the spot the vic played on Thursday nights. Gus' was a small establishment and always kept the mood right as R&B played from the jukebox.

But to fully appreciate what this place offered, you first had to recognize that this was a local favorite which meant you had to be used to dancing and dining, and they had more to offer than just wings and fries. They had bomb burgers, ribs, and chop steak during the day. And if you saved room for dessert, you could cop some sweet Japanese pastry called Manju, plus peach and pineapple turnovers that would turn you over.

Ahmad positioned himself to get a better view of the club's entrance. He watched females of all shapes and ethnicities squeeze into the club. But one in particular piqued his interest. Ahmad figured she was around five-five, but about five-eleven with the heels on her red bottoms.

From where he stood, he could tell she was caramel complected with long black hair. She had full breasts, and an ass that could give K Michelle a run for her money. Ahmad recognized her, but didn't know where from. But that no longer mattered, as Ahmad snapped back to reality. Just a few paces behind the eyes candy Ahmad spotted his man. A brown skinned brother entered the club right behind the female Ahmad was eyeing. Gazing down at his Cartier, he was able to see that it was a quarter til one, which meant he had a little wait before his mission would be complete.

So Ahmad walked back down the block and hopped in his whip. He turned the ignition not quite the entire way, flicked the high beams once, then the windshield wipers and watched as the hidden compartment under the glove box opened. The compartment held just enough space for his black and gray P89. Ahmad grabbed the gun, only to admire it for a second. He then hit a button on the left side, just above the handle and the clip slid down. He double checked but already knew the clip's content.

Ahmad was still slouched over the bench seat when he noticed headlights in the side mirror pulling up right behind him. He quickly secured the hidden compartment back in hiding and took the gun off safety. The lights on the vehicle turned off. The passenger door opened and a female stepped out. She was average height, slender, with okay facial features. She groped about clumsily in her purse until she retrieved what looked to be a cell phone. From the rearview, Ahmad noticed two more figures stepping from the driver's side. They slowly walked pass. After they were all in view, Ahmad let out a sigh of relief. *False alarm!* The trio's only interests was clubbing. But in the streets, Ahmad knew he could never be too cautious.

Reaching into the ashtray, he retrieved his half smoked blunt, put a new flame to it, and leaned back. As he rolled back, so did his eyes. He exhaled the piff, all in one motion. The smoke sifted through the car, and Ahmad inhaled another deep pull, enjoying the effects. His head was tilted on the headrest, and his eyes were wide shut.

Ahmad periodically zoned out, much of it stemming from the loss of his brother and comrade. He and Bobby had grown up together in the Southside's Village projects. They were your typical kids growing up in the *Jungle*, with dreams of making it out that ghetto. But with their playground being headquarters to hustlers, gunmen and knucklers, they learned early on just how vicious the streets of York could be.

Police profiled folks because of their hues, junkies walked about zombielike, and death was never far away. *In the Jungle, any day could be your last.*

Both, Ahmad and Bobby became products of that environment. Skipping school, smoking blunts, stealing cars corrupted their adolescent years. Eventually they graduated to *the jux*. And once they saw how lucrative that was, it became their number one hustle. At least until Bobby's untimely demise.

Made in the USA
Middletown, DE
28 April 2023

29622869R00137